"I don't laugh anymor[e], [I've]
seen UFOs[.]"

Former President Jimmy Carter
ABC News January 22, 1999

"I believe that these extraterrestrial vehicles and their crews are visiting this planet from other planets."

Major Gordon Cooper – Mercury Astronaut

"We can't deny that, and the evidence points to the fact that, Roswell was a real incident, and that indeed an alien craft did crash, and that material was recovered from that crash site..."

Astronaut Dr. Edgar Mitchell, Apollo 14 Mission

"It is time for the truth to be brought out in open Congressional hearings. Behind the scenes, high-ranking Air Force officers are soberly concerned about the UFOs. But, through official secrecy and ridicule, many citizens are lead to believe the unknown flying objects are nonsense. To hide the facts, the Air Force has silenced its personnel."

Former Director of Central Intelligence,
Vice Admiral R.H. Hillenkoetter
The New York Times,
Sunday, February 28, 1960

LUPO

CONVERSATIONS WITH AN E.T.

by
Louise Rose Aveni

the Peppertree Press
Sarasota, Florida

Disclaimer

This book was written as a work of fiction and, as such, any resemblance to persons living or dead is strictly the result of intertwining a compilation of personalities with the author's artistic creativity.

Cover Design and Interior Book Design by Vernon Firestone

Copyright © 2007 by Louise Aveni
All rights reserved. Published by the Peppertree Press, LLC.

the Peppertree Press and associated logos are trademarks of the Peppertree Press, LLC.

No part of this publication may be reproduced, stored in a retrieval system, transmitted in any form or by any means, electronic, mechanical, photocopying, recording, or otherwise, without prior written permission of the publisher and author/illustrator.
For information regarding permissions, write to
the Peppertree Press, LLC., Attention: Publisher, 4017 Swift Road, Sarasota, FL 34231.

ISBN: 978-1-934246-28-3
Library of Congress Number: Cataloging-in-Publication Data
Printed in the U.S.A.
Printed March, 2007

Table Of Contents

Author's Note	vii
Dedication	ix
A Word of Thanks	xi
Prologue	xiii
Stephan	1
Leaving Paradise	15
Coming to America	29
The Shrink	41
Back on the Farm	56
The Other E.T.	61
Nathan	70
Sedona	77
They're Here!	86
The Lobbyist	99
Lions and Tigers and Bears, Oh My!	105
Lupo Speaks	110
Imagine	123
Epilogue	132

*Why shouldn't truth be stranger than fiction?
Fiction, after all, has to make sense.*

– Mark Twain

Author's Note

As we embrace the new dawning of the Age of Aquarius, taking another quantum leap into the acceptance of other beings, new dimensions, and spiritual realms, life on other planets holds the portent of an infinite number of possibilities.

No longer is this subject taboo. Quite the opposite. The human race, as we have come to perceive it, is not only reaching for the stars for answers but going inward on a parallel quest for truth.

You are about to embark on a literary journey into one of those infinite possibilities. The determination of its validity lies deep within the reader's soul. Only *you* can decide what rings as truth to you.

After all ... what is unseen by some... is realty and experience for others.

*To Mom and Dad and to all those in spirit
who know the truth*

A Word Of Thanks

This has been such an amazing journey and one I have not had to travel alone. So it is then, that I take this opportunity to give thanks to those special spirits both in physical and non-physical who have guided me, supported me, and encouraged me along the way. Without them, this literary effort would not have been possible.

To Tom: Many thanks for sharing your wisdom and insight and providing me with the courage to continue my literary quest by sharing your amazing stories and showing me your photographic evidence to the government's contrary. The time *has* come!

To Vicki: How can I ever thank you enough for providing me with temporary safe haven and the magical space to write the majority of this epic. I love you beyond words.

To my dear, dear friends from "A" to "Z" who believe in me and have the uncanny ability to keep me grounded, yet let me fly and dream, all at the same time. I am forever grateful and feel eternally blessed to have you in my experience. Nameste!

To my wonderful publisher, Julie Ann Howell, editor Angie Jones and my fabulous cover designer, Vern Firestone, for capturing the true essence of my literary intention by enveloping my story with your creative genius - many, many thanks!

Finally, to my angels, guides and other beings who've led the way, provided the inspirational words, not to mention the fortitude to never give up. This is a story that needed to be told and now *They* are grateful.

Prologue

Somewhere in the foothills of the Matterhorn, just over the border of the Italian Alps, a small child races frantically into the cold, dark autumn night as the cries of wolves echo in the distance.

Stephan, barely three years old, cries out as, in haste, his delicate skin is pricked and scratched by low-lying brush that obstructs his flight. His ebony eyes are wide in full dilation to receive what little moonlight filters through the thicketed forest. All the while, his chest heaves to retain the breath that will lurch him forward even further into the night.

Distant voices call out to him, but he does not answer. Stopping only long enough to catch his breath, this desperate child of the night darts off in yet another random direction with no apparent course or destination.

The wolves' cries are ever closer while those of the humans are swallowed up in the abyss behind him.

Running harder now, he cannot stop, must not stop. He races blindly deeper into the forest in an attempt to secure safe haven, but from whom or from what? For all along, hasn't his course been deliberately set not in the direction of the voices that implore his response ... but away from them?

Growing weary, he slows his pace. Fatigue now betrays his young muscles as the terrain beneath his tender feet becomes mountainous.

Faltering at each effort of every step, he suddenly trips, falling in slow motion over a large unseen tree root. Before he can cry out in pain, the sounds of something moving in the nearby brush force him to cover his mouth, stifling the scream that waits within.

His concentration is now on the sound of breathing, albeit not his own. For he has all but stopped breathing in anticipation of what lurks nearby.

A twig snaps. He gasps another silent breath as his eyes train their focus on the immense yellow eyes that watch him from the surrounding brush.

Too young to gauge what would seem to others an eternity, he watches the creature slowly and stealthfully emerge from the darkness into the moonlight, where its identity is no longer a mystery.

Stephan shouts excitedly, "Lupo!" and as if returning the greeting, the large brown-and-gray wolf tilts its head as it approaches the boy.

Stephan

I was born in a Catholic hospital on February 10, 1957, in Varese, Italy, a little border town between Italy and Switzerland.

Shortly after my birth, I was placed in an orphanage in Milan, Italy. My earth name is Stephan (pronounced Ste-phan), last name, not important.

I never knew my mother or my father. Actually, I was kept from any knowledge of them for my own protection, I was told.

I was raised the first few years of my life in foster homes. My first recollection of anything in my childhood was as a small boy at the age of three years, and my special visitors, which, I later figured out, were E.T.'s (extraterrestrials).

I was living with a foster family on a farm situated on a mountain plateau in the highlands. In those days, farmhouses in Europe were structured literally like forts, with the animals kept in stalls around the perimeter of a rectangular courtyard, while the family resided on an upper level accessed by a surrounding deck or catwalk.

This design had been used successfully for centuries in an effort to ward off any persons who might entertain thoughts of stealing the livestock or causing harm to the residing families. They were literal fortresses.

I adored this place. It was a natural playground for a three-year-old boy, with its friendly trees to climb and soft, clay earth, perfect for making mud pies.

I vividly recall riding on tractors, digging ditches with my plastic gardening tools, and, best of all, not being scolded for getting dirty. Even now, if I close my eyes, I can totally recall the images and the fragrance of the rich brown earth, the clarity of the brilliant blue sky with majestic snow-capped mountains as a backdrop. For all intents and purposes, this was my heaven on earth. I never wanted to leave this place.

At a very early age, I began what my elders referred to as sleepwalking. In fact, I would even say it became one of my specialties. One night, in particular, while taking one of my "evening strolls," I saw three unusual-looking beings on the catwalk of our living quarters. One of the beings was taller than the other two and, strange as it may sound, I clearly remember not feeling any fear and, more importantly, I experienced an instant sense of peace and familiarity in their presence.

I must admit I can't recall actually speaking with them, at least not in the traditional way, but we did share a dialogue of sorts, an exchange of another kind that validated they were, indeed, there before me and meant me no harm.

In Italy in the evening hours, the farmers were terrified of Lupo, which is Italian for "wolf." If one was spotted in the area, you could hear cries of "Lupo! Lupo!" — which was the equivalent of someone yelling, "Fire! Fire!" It drew the same response from the other farmers and their families. My reaction, however, was vastly different. I was an animal lover, and the innocent child in me considered Lupo my friend, much to the dismay of my foster family.

Because I was so young, I threw caution to the wind and would often wander off the confines of the hillside farm and run among the creatures of the forest. As a matter of fact, one night I found myself blindly compelled to venture out into the darkness in search of Lupo. I had absolutely no fear, so I defiantly left the security

LUPO: CONVERSATIONS WITH AN E.T.

of the fortress to find my "friends" and Lupo. I can tell you, this was viewed by others as strange behavior and only the beginning for me of what would be conceived as chronic dysfunctional behavior.

But I'll also tell you, that night forever changed the way I looked at this illusion called life. In some strange, unexplainable way I knew I was not from this place called Italy. In fact, more often than not my gaze drifted skyward, searching and waiting. For what, you ask? I really didn't know at the time, but later it was made crystal clear to me.

Many years later I discovered through a casual reading of an article relating to UFO sightings in Italy that E.T.'s (extraterrestrials) were referred to as "Lupo." At that moment, the pieces of my personal human puzzle began to take shape, providing me with a hint of understanding toward my magnetic draw to Lupo and the unearthly visitors I encountered there on the catwalk.

ॐ

(Flashback)

Young Stephan bolts upright in his makeshift bed that was built on uneven slats of wood harvested from nearby trees surrounding his home, his *Castle in the Clouds* as he would later refer to it.

His crude mattress was formed out of a combination of old blankets and hay that smells of the livestock housed in the courtyard fortress below. And yet, quite comfortable, at least for a small three-year-old body.

His bed, an addition to the three others that form the "dormitory" where he and his foster brothers sleep, is positioned nearest the bedroom door as reassurance for the toddler who finds great comfort being one step closer in proximity to MaMa and PaPa, his foster parents.

What was it that startled him out of his slumber? Was there a noise? Did anyone else hear it? He guesses not as the others lay deep asleep. The only sounds are the steady rhythmic inhales and exhales of the family as they show no signs of acknowledgment that anything out of the ordinary is afoot.

Stephan remains in a heightened state of alertness as he cocks his head first in one direction, then another. His tiny ears listening … listening. There it is again!

Now, with intense curiosity and total abandon, he throws back his coverlet in one long, effortless motion and places his small bare feet onto the cold wooden floor.

Garbed only in his flannel nightshirt, even his slight frame causes the wooden floor planks to creak and moan as he pads his way across the dormitory. But the sounds go unnoticed by his roommates as they continue their slumber.

With the stealth of a cat, Stephan works his way silently to the nearby doorway of the living quarters, then tiptoes through the kitchen area until he finally spies the outline of the door that leads out onto the catwalk.

His focus is temporarily diverted to a bright illumination that spills through a window into the kitchen, giving it the appearance of midday. This brief interruption is quickly forgotten, however, as he becomes totally engrossed in continuing his exploration of the mysterious sound that jolted him from his slumber.

Even on tiptoe, Stephan is barely able to reach the door latch with his small hands. He carefully opens the door with slow, deliberate intent so as not to wake the others.

Stepping out onto the catwalk, he is blinded by a light so bright that his immediate reaction is to cover his eyes with both hands, peeking only between his fingers as his eyes begin to adjust. Standing just outside the door now, he takes in a sharp, quick breath of crisp cold air and releases a body shiver in an attempt to deal with the frigid outside temperature.

The illumination spotlights the courtyard below, exposing the livestock as they, too, remain undisturbed in their sleep. Taking a moment to notice the fog that emits from his mouth as his warm breath hits the cold air, Stephan wonders if the bright light means it's morning and, if so, why hasn't the rest of the family gotten up yet. As his eyes make their final adjustment, he scans the sky, only to discover the twinkling mass of stars that tell him it is, indeed, still nighttime. Then he sees it! The brilliance of the full harvest moon is the source of all this light.

Startled by another noise that seems to come from close behind him, Stephan takes in another gasp of air almost too painful to inhale. His eyes now in full expansion strain to bring into focus the shapes that are approaching. He wonders … is someone really there? The question is no sooner thought than answered — *Yes! Someone or something is there before him!*

First he sees one, …then two … no three! Three shapes coming ever closer to where he stands all alone on the catwalk. Two of the figures appear small — like him — while the third shape is much taller and appears to be standing behind the smaller ones as if introducing them to him, but without a sound.

They stand before him, their thin, barely there lips not moving; no audible words are exchanged; he only "hears" them in his head. How do they do that? he wonders.

For some unknown reason, Stephan doesn't fear these strange beings, nor does he any longer notice the cold night air that a moment before had him wishing he were warm and cozy in his dormitory bed.

A smile begins to form on Stephan's face as the trio moves ever closer; all the while a low humming sound begins to swell onto the catwalk, until its vibration permeates all that surrounds him, then — suddenly — there is nothing but complete dark silence.

The next thing Stephan knows is that he is back in his bed. He is snuggled deep beneath his blankets. Lying still, eyes blinking furiously, he wonders ... did that really happen? Was I having a dream? He quickly decides it was real — at least, to *this* three-year-old it was.

The crowing of the rooster in the courtyard far below officially announces the start of a new day. As the family rises one by one and begins moving about in preparation for breakfast and the daily chores ahead, Stephan bounds out of bed chattering in earnest all the while MaMa, his foster mother, attempts to remove his night clothing and dress him for the day.

As MaMa continues her struggle with an excited wriggling toddler, Stephan continues to chatter on and on about how ... *first* there was a loud noise that woke him ... then there was the *big bright light* ... then how *very, very cold* the air was outside ... and then — the very best part that he has saved for last — there were those *three beings* coming toward him on the catwalk!

"What? What are you talking about, Stephan?" chirps Antonio, who at age nine is the eldest of the farmer's children and also one of his dormitory roommates. As MaMa pulls the warm crimson sweater she knitted for Stephan over his head, his muffled reply is soon dismissed as nothing more than a toddler's ramblings of a dream he must have had last night. The other two roommates, Vincent, age seven, and Franco, age five, giggle openly as they tease Stephan about his wild imagination while Stephan professes that this really, *really* did happen!

Overhearing this conversation, PaPa, who is in the nearby kitchen pouring himself his first container of hot coffee, is disturbed by Stephan's reporting and begins to scold him about wandering about into the night. The giggles and the chiding directed at Stephan from the children continue until PaPa, now standing before them obviously upset, brings a halt to the morning chaos and immediate silence to their mocking as he speaks in a more urgent tone.

LUPO: CONVERSATIONS WITH AN E.T.

The children freeze-frame to their spots and listen obediently as PaPa continues his lecture. He reminds all of them to *never* venture into the dark without an adult and how there are hidden dangers that lurk in the nearby woods, in particular, Lupo!

"There will be no more of this foolishness, Stephan. Do you understand? The other children know better and now, so do you!" he finishes with complete command.

Lecture now over, the brood finds it safe to unglue themselves from their fixed positions. They scramble to the kitchen table to devour the breakfast breads, whose sweet aromas have been wafting through the house since dawn.

As MaMa pours more hot coffee for PaPa and fresh goat's milk for the children, the talk soon turns to the chores ahead. There is no more mention of Stephan's wanderings. At least not today.

It is late fall and that means harvest time, even though the crop is barely large enough to accommodate the family's needs through the long, cold winter ahead. So life on the hillside farm continues as normal.

Normal. What an unusual word. What is normal anyway? Certainly what was thought of as normal no longer exists for young Stephan. He has a new normal as his nighttime visitations with his unusual friends continue in the weeks that follow. Only now, he no longer talks about these exciting encounters with anyone for fear of receiving another scolding. So they continue in silence.

He frolics with the farmer's children by day and his "other" playmates by night. Unlike most children at bedtime whose customary resistance is expected, Stephan has become unusually cooperative. His anticipation of playtime with his *friends* and all the new sights he'll see have him enthusiastically scurrying off to his bed.

Then one stormy afternoon it all changes. An early approaching snowstorm keeps Stephan and the other children from their outside activities. They are made to stay indoors while PaPa hastens to finish his chores and prepare for the impending storm before nightfall.

While Antonio is off in a corner reading one of his favorite adventure books, young Vincent, Franco, and Stephan are all at the kitchen table quietly drawing and coloring, exploring their imaginations on paper. Like most toddlers, Stephan can amuse himself for hours on end drawing on scraps of paper he has liberated from one source or another.

MaMa hums to herself as she stands at the stove preparing the evening meal, content that her family is warm and well. Curious about Stephan's intense focus on his doodling, she stops stirring dinner just long enough to glance over her shoulder and with sincere interest asks, "What's that you're drawing, Stephan?"

Vincent and Franco, totally immersed in their own creations, have not yet eyed Stephan's rendering. In typical childlike fashion, Stephan sees no need for description and proudly holds up the yet unfinished work of art.

Suddenly, the ladle once held in MaMa's hand crashes noisily to the floor, startling not only Stephan but Vincent and Franco, who shriek in surprise. With shaking knees, MaMa begins her slow, uncertain steps toward Stephan. Her mouth agape, eyes wide, not believing nor fully comprehending how a child as young as Stephan could create such an etching.

"What ...what's th.... what is this, Stephan?" MaMa pleads.

Hearing the commotion, Antonio enters the kitchen, with an open book still clutched in his hands, and asks what all the noise is about? With unhesitant candor, Stephan spews out his description of the picture. The other children begin to laugh and mock Stephan but are quickly silenced when they note MaMa's reaction to the drawing.

Stephan wishes he hadn't been so eager to share these images as he unsteadily begins his explanation. "It's a ship

… It's the inside of one of the ships I ride in with my … my friends … you know, like the ones up in the sky … like …" he trails off barely audible.

Without warning, MaMa snatches the drawing from his small hands and, with quivering voice, orders Stephan to his room until summoned. Not understanding the reason for this scolding, Stephan tearfully jumps off the kitchen stool where, just moments before, he sketched in reverie.

Not long after being exiled to his room, Stephan hears PaPa enter the kitchen, loudly stomping the snow off his boots as he prattles on to anyone who will listen about his long, hard day's work. MaMa's still-hysterical voice begins to recount to PaPa the events as they unfolded just a few moments ago. Stephan clearly senses her disapproval and begins to fear what will happen next.

He quickly retreats to the safe haven of the underside of his bed. Barely able to catch his breath in his hasty retreat, he hears the familiar creaking of the dormitory door as it opens wide.

There stands PaPa larger than life, Stephan's drawing clutched in his large hands that are still covered in earth from the day's labor. "Stephan? … Stephan, it's all right. You can come out. Stephan, come to me," PaPa speaks without anger.

As Stephan's body involuntarily obeys the request, he emerges from underneath his bed with bowed head in slow approach. He fixes his eyes on the wood floor, not daring to raise them up to meet PaPa's gaze.

PaPa gently takes Stephan's small hand in his and leads him back into the kitchen where MaMa and the other children stare at him in silent, wide-eyed confusion.

Lifting Stephan high upon the same stool he occupied moments before, PaPa begins: "Stephan, what are these?"

Before answering, Stephan first glances at his foster mother then darts his eyes quickly back to PaPa, who now more urgently implores an explanation. Mumbling weakly at first, then, at PaPa's prompting, Stephan recites the exact same reply he provided MaMa a short while ago. To everyone's amazement, PaPa turns and, in silent disbelief, retreats out the front door, down the stairs from the catwalk into the courtyard below, still clutching Stephan's artwork.

MaMa's eyes are now red and swollen from her own tears as she follows her husband's retreat leaving Stephan high upon his stool, with Antonio, Vincent, and Franco sitting around him, speechless to say the least.

So there he continues to sit listening intently, straining to understand the exchange of tones between his foster parents who are discussing what has just occurred. Vincent and Franco rush headlong to the kitchen window to, watch and wait for their parents' next action while Antonio stares blankly at Stephan.

Stephan begins to quiver with anticipation of the punishment sure to follow. With all his might, he can't seem to wrap his young mind around the reason why his drawing has brought about such anger from the two people he's come to love and depend upon.

Then he hears their footsteps on the catwalk and is immediately engulfed with renewed fear as the front door opens ever so slowly.

His foster parents re-enter the kitchen together with heads held low, and PaPa calmly instructs Stephan to wash up for dinner.

That's it? ... Go wash my hands? Without hesitation and before PaPa can change his mind, Stephan jumps off the stool and rushes to the sink in complete compliance. Much to his and the other children's amazement, there will be no punishment — just a sincere scolding from PaPa to never, never draw these images again, nor is he to speak of his nightly visitors, for it will no longer be tolerated.

Stephan retreats to his room until he is called for

dinner, grateful there will be no punishment, but the fact that his artwork has brought about such a powerful reprimand confuses Stephan all the more.

After all, his new friends mean no harm. They take him to magical places in strange soundless vehicles. They talk without moving their lips. How do they do that, anyway? he still ponders.

It makes no sense to Stephan that he'll never be allowed to do this again. He does, however, know one thing for sure: he *must* obey his foster parents because he likes it here. He doesn't want to make PaPa or MaMa upset with him again. Enough said.

The sun has set and PaPa has lit a warm, inviting fire in the hearth. Dinner is ready but Stephan barely touches his food, all the while a single tear falls silently from his cheek onto his plate. The jeers and covered-mouth giggles from the other children are but another reminder of how different and separate he is beginning to feel from them. He has yet to discover that he possess a higher-than-average intelligence with a superior comprehension level, and that he thinks, speaks, and acts like a child far beyond his years, which will soon become an issue for those who don't understand.

Emotionally exhausted, Stephan takes himself to bed in grateful anticipation of sleep and the refuge he will most certainly find there. Sleep comes swift and deep. Deeper and deeper he goes as he is lulled by a soft, low humming sound that beckons him further into blissful slumber.

The next thing he's aware of is that he is running — no racing — through the freezing night, dressed only in his flannel nightshirt and warm woolen socks, grateful that his feet are somewhat protected from the rough terrain.

Voices call his name from a distance. Is he dreaming again? Is this real? Regardless of the answer, Stephan presses forward as fast as his small legs can manage.

Stopping only long enough to catch his breath, this

desperate child of the night darts off in yet another random direction with no apparent course or destination.

The wolves' cries are ever closer while those of the humans are swallowed up in the abyss behind him.

Running harder now, he cannot stop, must not stop. He races blindly deeper and deeper into the forest in an attempt to secure safe haven, but from whom or from what? For all along, hasn't his course been deliberately set not in the direction of the voices that implore his response ... but away from them?

Growing weary, his pace slows. Fatigue now betrays his young muscles as the terrain beneath his tender feet becomes mountainous.

Faltering at each effort of every step, he suddenly trips, falling in slow motion over a large unseen tree root. Before he can cry out in pain, the sounds of something moving in the nearby brush force him to cover his mouth, stifling the scream that waits within.

His concentration is now on the sound of breathing, albeit not his own. For he has all but stopped breathing in anticipation of what lurks nearby.

A twig snaps. He gasps another silent breath as his large ebony eyes train their focus on the immense yellow eyes that watch him from the surrounding brush.

Too young to gauge what would seem to others an eternity, he watches the creature slowly and stealthfully emerge from the darkness into the moonlight, where its identity is no longer a mystery.

Stephan shouts excitedly, "Lupo!" and as if returning the greeting, the large brown-and-gray wolf tilts its head as it approaches the boy.

Chest heaving, tears flowing freely down his face, all Stephan can manage to blurt out is "Lupo! Lupo, I am so glad to see you!"

Lupo excitedly licks Stephan's tear-stained face as he

prances about the boy's small body with gentle bumps and nudges in welcome. When Stephan finally calms a bit, Lupo indicates for the boy to follow him. He leads Stephan to a cave opening, deep within the thicket, where they'll be safe and a bit warmer, at least for a while.

Lupo's tongue is extended as he, too, reaches to catch his own panting breath. While stroking Lupo's thick fur, Stephan begins to stare into his friend's large yellow eyes. A low, barely audible humming vibrates all around them as they begin to exchange their unspoken thoughts.

Here they sit, this unlikely duo, caught up only in each other's gaze. Their breathing is now jointly paced at a remarkably slow rate. Not a sound is uttered as Stephan willingly becomes the receiver of unearthly knowledge and wisdom. For he has been chosen and must comply with the instructions being imprinted upon his young superior brain.

As the cold night air brings a shiver to Stephan's small body, his fixed gaze with Lupo is broken. Feeling that it is time to return home, Stephan reaches up to Lupo's thick, furry neck for one last embrace. A solitary tear falls from Stephan's eyes onto Lupo's extended paw in farewell … at least for now.

As Stephan rises to start his journey home he turns around to look back one more time upon his friend, but Lupo is gone.

Once again, Stephan becomes aware of the voices calling in the night. Only this time, instead of going away from them, he moves deliberately toward them.

Not long into his weary walk back, he is suddenly blinded by a single light that shines directly into his eyes, and met with, "Here he is! I've found him!"

Before he can regain his vision from the blinding flashlight, Stephan is swept up into the billowing arms of PaPa, who speaks not a word as he firmly, yet gently, carries him back through the blackness of the forest to the warmth and comfort of their hillside farm.

Though the dim cast of light is barely enough to guide the searcher's' way home, it is enough to expose PaPa's grateful tears streaming down his otherwise rugged face. His breathing is quick and shallow as he trudges through the darkened forest, ducking barely visible tree limbs as he aims toward the light of the farm with Stephan cradled closely against his chest.

MaMa is perched anxiously atop the catwalk, wrapped only in a bed cloth, scanning the dark outline of the woods for any sign of PaPa and the others.

Then she spots them! The wavering beams from their searchlights broadcast their return. Silently she prays they were successful in finding their tiny charge unharmed. Her heart all but stops when first she sees her husband emerge from the woods as she squints to make out the form he holds close to him. As she spies the outline of Stephan's curly locks, she emits a loud cry of gratitude to God and the others for their unselfish efforts in bringing Stephan home safe.

MaMa races frantically down the catwalk, barely touching each tread. Armed with an extra blanket in her hands, she dashes to meet PaPa and Stephan as the other children watch and cheer from the kitchen window above.

Once inside, PaPa gingerly carries Stephan to his bed and lays the boy upon his pillow, gently stroking his head in silent thanks for his safe return. Stephan quickly falls into a deep, silent slumber despite MaMa's urgent efforts to remove his torn clothing and socks filled with earth and twigs. It feels good to be back in his Castle in the Clouds. He'll sleep well now.

Leaving Paradise

I was taken away from my mountain paradise after a year's residence, certainly not because of my one-time misjudgment of running off into the night. At least, that's what I was told. Perhaps in those days it was thought best to not get too attached to a foster child for fear of traumatic repercussions for both child and foster family.

At any rate, I was moved to another foster home in the city of Milan, Italy. This was not a happy experience for me. This new family was using the welfare system to subsidize their income by taking in foster children. The allotments given to them for clothing and food for my benefit were redirected to their own four children.

I was not really cared for. I was a non-entity to them, a ghost figure forced to drink sour goat's milk and eat stale bread while their own children feasted on fresh eggs and meats.

But the ultimate abuse was of a more physical nature. In an effort to keep me from sleepwalking, I was tied up in a closet each night. This was done to ensure they would not lose their subsidy should I suddenly disappear and not return.

I was always being accused of trying to run away, when in reality what I believe to be true was that I was being taken by E.T.'s for programming, training, or scientific experiments. Because of my young age, I wasn't always able to remember what was happening *during those sleepwalks. Or perhaps, most likely, programmed to forget.*

Finally, at age four and a half, I was chosen by my adoptive parents, who were living in the United States.

Once earmarked for adoption, I was moved out of the foster home and placed back into the same orphanage until the adoption could be completed.

Unfortunately, I was to discover that this, too, was not a good place at all. Here I was, a little country boy thrown in with all these city children — not to mention my highly active psychic prowess and nighttime excursions; well, you can just imagine the level of disruption this produced.

I was beginning to learn that fear brings about many types of reactionary results. So as a direct result of my sleepwalking, I would get daily beatings, mostly in the mornings, from some of the older children, as they were the ones who saw the evidence of my "relocation."

When I would have a visitation — I hesitate to use the word "abduction" here — I would be returned to the proximity of the area of my departure, to within eight to ten feet. This could sometimes mean the difference between being inside or outside a building. So if, for example, they found me in the courtyard when all the doors and windows had been secured the night before, it left them with no alternative but to deem me a clever escape artist.

When questioned by the nuns at the orphanage as to how I got outside, my emphatic explanation of E.T. or angel visitations was not met with any kind of support or, at the very least, feigned understanding. It was viewed as pure fabrication and dealt with harshly.

There was one older boy in particular, the typical bully who found great delight in tormenting me in whatever way he could.

Finally one day, I'd had enough! In an effort to bring about what I thought would be an end to his constant abuse, I boldly confronted him, punched him in his stomach — as that was the only area I could reach, given my small stature — and then ran like the devil. When this bully recovered from the shock of my retribution, he immediately began his sincere pursuit. As a result of this mad chase, I injured my arm requiring immediate medical attention.

Ultimately, all this did was delay my adoption and immigration to the United States. No clear winner here! My convalescence lasted two whole months.

When I returned to the orphanage with my arm still in a cast, the first chance I got, I hit this bully over the head with it. Of course, this meant my arm needed to be reset, due to the reinjury caused by my revenge thus delaying, yet again, my journey to the United States and my adopted family. Was it worth it you ask? … (smiling).

ॐ

(Flashback)

Morning comes and Stephan awakes feeling quite groggy yet resolved to secretly follow Lupo's unspoken directives. He hears voices coming from the nearby kitchen, but he soon becomes aware of a male voice he doesn't recognize.

As he slowly climbs out of bed, his little legs and feet ache from his nighttime trek. He cautiously opens the bedroom door in an effort to peek into the kitchen and identify the source of this new voice, undetected. He notices the other children have already gotten up and are most likely off doing chores. They must have let him sleep. Not being able to see beyond the small crack of his bedroom door, he chooses to open it wide. Rubbing his eyes as he enters the kitchen area, MaMa speaks his name softly as she approaches him and leads him to join PaPa and the stranger sitting at the kitchen table.

"Stephan," PaPa begins in a gentle voice, "this is Mr. Mastriano. He runs an orphanage in a city not far from here called Milan. He is here to bring you to Milan to another home where there will be other children like you waiting to find a permanent family to live with. Until then, the orphanage will be your new home ..." PaPa's voice trails off, holding back his emotions as he finds the words difficult to form.

New home? I don't want a new home! I like it here! PaPa, MaMa, and the others are here! Lupo is here! Stephan shouts inside himself.

Then Stephan finds his voice and pleads to PaPa, MaMa, or anyone who will listen, "I won't be bad anymore! I won't walk in the night again! I won't run away again!" He leaps into the safety of PaPa's lap, all the while pleading for another chance.

"This is not a punishment, Stephan. MaMa and I are allowed to care for children who not our own for only a short time or until Mr. Mastriano finds a permanent home for them. Mr. Mastriano is here because he has found you a new home in America." PaPa explains.

America! Stephan has never heard of America. "Where is America? Is it nearby? Can I see you and MaMa and the other children?" Stephan's quivering voice pleads. PaPa's reply is little comfort for a young boy who barely knows the limited surroundings of his hillside home, with the exception of his nightly excursions with his "friends."

Struggling to contain his emotions, PaPa slowly rises with Stephan still in his arms and places him solidly onto his own stool then turns his head away as he explains, while pacing back and forth in the kitchen, that America is far away across a great sea and that they will not, most likely, see each other again.

By now, MaMa has also turned away, clearing the table of breakfast dishes in a futile effort to hide her free-flowing tears.

Stephan hesitates but a moment, then to everyone's amazement he wipes away his own tears as he softly and calmly asks, "When do I have to go?"

PaPa's reply is barely audible, "Right away, my boy … right away."

Packing up what few belongings he has acquired in his short life and brief stay with his hillside family, Stephan sees that MaMa has prepared a basket of food for their long journey to the city of Milan.

By now the other children, curious about whose car is on their land and what the stranger is doing here, begin to filter into the kitchen one behind the other. Antonio notices Stephan is carrying his belongings under his small arms while his mother hands the basket of food to Mr. Mastriano.

At the quiet urgings of the other children, Antonio finds the courage to ask PaPa what's going on. As he hesitantly recounts the situation at hand, his children gasp at the reality of Stephan's immediate departure.

While it's true they occasionally enjoy taunting Stephan when it comes to his imaginary friends and his outrageous talk of flying off in a space ship somewhere, they have all grown quite fond of their smallest roommate. Though they're no strangers to the comings and goings of other foster children left in their parents' temporary care, somehow Stephan, despite his abnormalities, has become one of them, and they know his departure will leave a void that won't readily be filled.

One by one, the farmer's children approach Stephan with half embraces and childlike mumblings about how he will be missed and how exciting for him that he'll soon be in a new home.

With nothing more to be said, they all solemnly process down the catwalk stairs. Stephan is led to take his seat in the back of Mr. Mastriano's car, and locks his gaze with PaPa's as he settles into his fate. As the car slowly drives away Stephan's last image is of his family waving in silent resignation as he journeys away from their lives and away from his beloved

LUPO: CONVERSATIONS WITH AN E.T.

Lupo.

The trip to Milan is long, and they stop only to partake of the delicious fixin's of chicken drumsticks, sweet bread, homemade grape juice from the farmer's vineyard, and — Stephan's personal favorite — fig squares that MaMa would bake at his insistence.

Night is falling and Stephan finds it nearly impossible to keep his eyes open. But open they stay as he has never traveled this road before, and his curiosity about the city betrays his body's urgent need for rest. Then he sees it! The lights of the city twinkle before him, announcing their impending arrival to his new life.

In typical kid fashion, Stephan excitedly asks Mr. Mastriano, "Are we there yet?" Mr. Mastriano's reply is gentle and engaging: "Soon," he informs Stephan, "very soon."

So many buildings, Stephan thinks, and they're all right next to each other! Where do they keep their goats and chickens and cows, he ponders.

The car comes to a halt and Stephan has, at last, reached his next destination. Mr. Mastriano helps him out of the car and leads him up a long set of stairs that mark the entrance to an old, dark, towering building, then through a huge doorway that leads yet again to another long and winding staircase. Once at the top of the stairs, Mr. Mastriano is greeted by Sister Marguerite, an unfriendly soul who immediately commandeers Stephan and his belongings and drags him to his new dormitory filled with dozens of sleeping children.

As Stephan is led to where he will sleep, Sister Marguerite tells him in a low, firm voice that he is to go right to sleep and not stir until the morning bell is rung. Stephan, now terrified of this gruff woman, nods his head in acknowledgment and climbs thankfully into his bed, where he quickly falls asleep.

The very next morning Stephan is awakened, not by the bell Sister Marguerite warned him about but by dozens of sets of strange eyes peering, closely watching his every move as he awakes.

Then it happens ... "GONG! GONG! GONG!" The continuous loud ringing of the bell. "G-O-N-G! G-O-N-G! G-O-N-G!"

All the other children scramble in chaos to dress and line up by the dormitory doorway and wait. But wait for what?

Then Sister Marguerite appears, along with another lady dressed in the same funny clothing. Heads covered in cloth hoods with long, flowing, layered skirts. But where are their hands? thinks Stephan. All he can see are their arms.

He has never seen a nun before and is not savvy to their demeanor or conditioned posture, standing and walking with their hands hidden beneath their habits. Stephan has been witness to a lot of strange beings and behaviors in his young life, so this is just one more.

He is quickly launched onto the floor by an older boy, who Stephan guesses to be around eight years old. At any rate, Stephan, who has slept in his clothing, falls in line behind another big boy. There he stands, barely awake, book ended by two towering older boys. He falls in step with the others as they are marched down the long winding staircase he climbed not that long ago, upon his arrival last evening.

They tread down another long, cold hallway with only the sound of their shuffling feet echoing off the walls.

As they approach two large doors, Stephan notices a lot more of the ladies in funny clothing leading other groups of children through the same doorway. Only these children are girls, and they are of all different ages, just like the boys in his room.

They are instructed to take their seats and be quiet. The children obey with a few exceptions, who are met with swift retribution for their disobedience.

Something smells good, really good! Stephan shouts,

"I'm hungry! Are we going to eat now?" This brings a mass unison of turned heads upon his small presence, and he immediately realizes it's best to stay quiet.

As the children take their respective seats, a bustle of activity surrounds the room. Platters of biscuits and hot cereals are brought to the tables by the ladies in the hooded dresses.

As Stephan and a few others begin to grab for their share, Sister Marguerite shouts a warning that no food is to be touched until the morning prayer of blessings has been said. The only prayers Stephan has ever heard were those of the farmer when he hit his hand with a hammer while mending fences surrounding the fortress. He thinks it went something like "For God sakes ... ," then he simply can't remember the rest.

Oh well, he can wait until he thanks God for bringing him such great-smelling food. Once the blessing is said, as the saying goes: let the games begin!

Stephan and the others take turns grabbing at biscuits and hold their glasses up to be filled with delicious, fresh goat's milk brought around by a nice lady in yet another funny-looking garb. Only she is much younger than the others and seems to enjoy serving the children and laughs along with them as they sputter out words of gleeful appreciation.

After the morning meal, Sister Marguerite informs the other children that Stephan is a new arrival, but he will be leaving later on during the day to be cared for by a local foster family willing to take his charge while he awaits his adoption. What is she talking about? Stephan wonders.

One of the older boys tells him how lucky he is to not have to stay in this place, and how he's been waiting for years to have a family outside of these walls to care for him.

Down deep Stephan does feel lucky. Lucky to have lived with PaPa, MaMa, and the other children in their *Castle in the Clouds*. Now he can only hope that his new family will care for him as well, and that he'll be happy once again in a wonderful new home until he goes to America.

Stephan is instructed to follow one of the nuns to Sister Marguerite's office. He is placed on a very hard wooden bench, where he sits and sits for what seems like an eternity, waiting for his foster family to pick him up.

Finally, a large man with a big belly and a small woman — with a belly to match his — bound through the door to Sister Marguerite's office.

They eye Stephan briefly and ask if this is the boy they are to care for. When answered in the affirmative, they quickly sign some papers, grab Stephan by the hand, and tell him to come with them.

"Stephan! My name is Stephan," he manages to utter as they whisk him into the hallway and out the front door, plopping him into the back seat of their tattered, smelly car.

Never casting a glance his way or a single kind word as they drive, this unlikely pair chatter away about things that have no meaning to Stephan. Soon they arrive at their destination and "… Stephan, is it? …" is told he can get out the car.

His belongings in hand, he follows their lead to an ugly house with no pretty flowers or shrubs or even any trees around it. A strange feeling rises up in Stephan's stomach — this may not be a very nice place.

At the front door they're greeted by the squeals of four children of varying ages, welcoming their parents home. They barely acknowledge Stephan as they jump in anticipation of what treats their parents have brought home for them. The parents, who apparently got an advance payment for Stephan's care, produce edible goodies for their children but neglect to share with Stephan.

This was the beginning of an unhappy experience with this foster family, who found a most clever way to take advantage of the system so as to provide their own family with food and clothing, leaving the foster children to fend for themselves.

Then it happens. Stephan's sleepwalking becomes a source of major irritation for this family, who are in dire fear of losing their meal ticket. So they decide the best course of action is to tie him up in a closet with just a blanket for warmth while they slumber comfortably in their own soft beds in their well-heated rooms.

The only relief Stephan experiences is during his nightly excursions with his *friends*, who take him to such amazing places and show him such incredible sights. At least, he is left with the feeling these visits take place. The truth of the matter is Stephan isn't sure himself anymore if these visits are real or not. Maybe he's supposed to forget. But one thing he is sure of: real or not, they are a welcome relief to his otherwise hostile state of being.

His waking hours are torturous, and he purposely avoids any contact or verbal exchange with any family members as he is sure to be beaten or punished for something that is either imagined or misunderstood. Even at the age of four and a half, he is smart enough to know it's best to be ignored by these people, for fear of retribution.

To the dismay of the foster family, Stephan's adoption is close to completion so he is returned, temporarily, to the orphanage in Milan while the appropriate paperwork is put in order, then it's off to America!

It has become a matter of the lesser of two evils for Stephan to either remain in an abusive foster home where he was neglected and forced to sleep in a closet or to experience the resumption of the orphanage's older boys' chastising and beatings that would surely follow his nightly disappearing acts.

So it is that Stephan readies himself for his new family in America and all the possibilities that lay before him in a new land.

As is the case with so many children, Stephan has a nemesis in the orphanage — an older boy named Michael, who is resentful of Stephan's cute appearance and, more now than ever, his opportunity to move out of this horrific place to begin a new life with a family in America.

After breakfast, Michael takes it upon himself to instigate yet another day of torture for Stephan. He continues his taunting by calling Stephan horrible names and by making spitballs out of paper while encouraging some of the others to assist in the assault at every opportunity.

Only this time, Stephan's had enough. He willfully confronts Michael while planning his escape to the girls' section of the play area, which is usually off limits to the boys.

Stephan releases a blow to Michael's midsection then runs as fast as his little legs can carry him to the safety of the girls' huge playhouse. Because he is still so small, he easily scales the exterior walls to the temporary safe haven of the roof.

All too soon, Michael, now in hot pursuit, reaches Stephan on the playhouse roof and pushes him, causing him to lose his balance and fall hard upon the concrete flooring, thus breaking his fragile little arm in two places.

The other children witnessing this fracas hysterically call for help, and one by one the nuns appear to clear the area and lend assistance to this fallen child. Stephan is taken to a nearby hospital for treatment, all the while being chastised by Sister Marguerite for his actions that, because of this injury, have set his adoption back a few months.

Because Stephan's injury is more severe than first thought, he is confined to bed-rest and a hospital stay of two months. Well, Stephan is not totally unhappy at this new prospect as he is guaranteed a respite from the beatings and the bullying, and in exchange will be well fed and cared for by the pretty nurses. Stephan finally has a break in the action, and, strangely enough, his visitations cease as well, if only for the short time he is in the hospital.

After his two-month recuperation, it is time to return to the orphanage. How Stephan has dreaded this day. However, this time he decides to take matters into his own hands by taking the offensive. Immediately upon his arrival, Stephan begins his own reign of terror by launching an unprovoked attack upon Michael's head with his cast, only to re-break his arm, thus setting back his adoption for the second time. America will have to wait … again!

Coming To America

In the fall of 1962, I finally made my way to America. I flew from Italy with an older boy named Demetrio, who was also being adopted by a family in this new land called America.

Neither one of us had ever flown in an airplane before. Demetrio was petrified, but I assured him it was all right. I instinctively knew what it would look like peering down on Earth. I had seen this view many times before, so I had no fear. At least, not until we landed, then I had plenty.

Here I was, barely five years old, in a strange land with a different language and going to live with people I had never met before. This was indeed a full plate for a young kid.

We flew into New York's LaGuardia Airport and were separated immediately. No time for goodbyes.

I was taken to meet my new family at the Angel Guardian Adoption Home in Long Island, New York, which was run by the Catholic Church. I don't mind telling you I was a very frightened little boy. I didn't want to be in America. I wanted only to return to my mountain home in Italy, with its peace and happy memories ... and Lupo.

I arrived wearing blue short pants with a red-and-white horizontal-striped shirt. I guess whoever dressed me thought these were very appropriate patriotic colors for my new country. I had no opinion on the matter.

Upon my arrival at Angel Guardian, I was greeted by two nuns who quickly removed my clothing, washed me down, combed my hair, then put new clothes on me. No more red, white and blue. Now, I was ready to meet my new parents.

When I was introduced to them, I felt no connection at first. But once I met my adopted mother's mother, who was a native Sicilian, the connection formed instantly, and a sense of well-being and acceptance began to work its way into my heart.

There were no other children in the home, and I remember not feeling particularly good about that. Being painfully shy and guarded, I spent my first few days imbedded in a corner of the living room, neither speaking nor listening to anyone.

Then a neighbor from across the street came over to get a glimpse of the new arrival. He was a shoe salesman who spoke not a word of Italian and, quite frankly, didn't even try, but for some unknown reason I felt a total affinity for him.

He would tease with me, and before long I was allowing myself to settle into the security of an environment that was, until that gifted moment, totally foreign to me. I give him total credit for those early moments of comfort and ease. His name was Shelby and he made me laugh — something I hadn't done in quite some time. It felt good. It felt very good.

A key factor to my instant bonding with Shelby may have been his bald-headed resemblance to my nighttime visitors. At any rate, he made sure I had the best shoes for my feet. I'd never owned a pair of sneakers before. Shelby made it his business — no, more his mission — to be sure I fit in with the other kids in the neighborhood.

My life was again beginning to change, but this time it was a welcome, comfortable change. It didn't take me very long to become a part of the neighborhood scene. There were children everywhere in my neighborhood. The houses surrounding my home were literally bursting at the seams with children.

The O'Malley family on one side of my house had eight

children; the Cochran family on the other side had seven, while the Geracci family directly across the street had four.

My life was showing signs of normalcy, whatever that was, and partly because I had learned the English language in literally two short weeks; I did not feel like the outsider any longer.

By now the neighborhood kids had started to call me Steffe, a nickname I grew to like and feel comfortable with as it denoted their acceptance of me into their fold. It was proof positive that I was one of them, had roots, and was part of the landscape. I liked that a lot!

I was considered exceptionally bright for my age, so much so that my parents decided to no longer hold back the speed of my induction into American culture.

So here I was at age five about to experience my first Halloween. My mother, who was a big Joe DiMaggio fan, dressed me up to look like him. Talk about waving the American flag and Mom's apple pie! This was truly the Americanization of Stephan, and my official initiation into Yankeedom.

Halloween was not a custom I had ever seen or heard of before, and yet it appealed to me greatly. While the other young children were frightened by the more gruesome costumes, I found the whole experience exciting — plus, don't forget all the candy I could carry at one time.

Of course, my mother would do the parent thing. You know, the part where you think you've got just about the most candy any kid could possibly conceive of in their possession at one time, then Mother says, "You can't eat this all now. You have to wait until after dinner."

I remember thinking, this is a dumb holiday. You go around for hours begging for candy just to have your mother say you can't eat it? I could only hope this American custom had some hidden meaning justifying the confiscation of my booty.

Tommy, a kid who lived two houses down from me, became my best friend. He had two older brothers — Matthew and Brian, who talked my mother into letting me go out after dinner for one more round of trick or treat. Well, of course as soon as we hit the street, Tommy's brothers took off with their friends, which left me, Tommy, and another neighbor boy named Daniel to explore the dank and dark recesses of the Halloween streets by ourselves.

This was a pretty special moment for any five-year-old — one we were not going to squander. We didn't particularly see ourselves as courageous kids, let alone old enough to roam the dark neighborhood unsupervised. And yet, the thought of the endless possibilities that crept into our young imaginations sparked a few nervous giggles, if not a sense of false courage.

As we were walking along the darkened streets, we looked up at the clear night sky and began talking about stars and stuff. I told them, "Look up there. See that bright star? That's where I'm from." I was pointing to Sirius, which shone the most brilliant blue in the night sky.

Sirius is located in the eye of the greater dog Canis Major and is only visible in the northern hemisphere from early fall until early spring ... but I could always find it. Sirius can easily be located by finding the three bright stars that form constellation Orion's belt. Just follow an imaginary line through these stars to Sirius, which was now just above the horizon.

Tommy and Daniel didn't show any particular reaction to my comment, other than saying something like "Are you kidding?" to which I replied, "No, I'm Sirius." I don't think they got my humor. All they knew was that I was foreign, I was not born where they were born, and that I kind of popped up out of nowhere — so the rest was pretty much accepted.

I told them I came here in a big silver flying machine — to them that meant a traditional airplane. Five-year-olds don't have much of a concept of countries, never mind galaxies. My friends were more intent on finding out what it was like where I came from.

My answer was always the same. With a finger pointed toward the heavens, I would always track the exact same star. It didn't matter that I couldn't explain anything else about Sirius. It was enough for me, and apparently for them.

ॐ

(Flashback)

Stephan stands quietly beside the stewardess as she scans the mass of strange faces whizzing by. She anticipates the handing off of her young charge to the next relayer on Stephan's journey to his new home in America.

At last, a young woman dressed in the same funny clothing the nuns wore in Italy approaches the stewardess and identifies herself as the emissary sent to escort young Stephan to his next stop — the Angel Guardian Adoption Home in Long Island, New York. With the word "Angel" in the adoption home's name, he's counting on it being a good place to stay while he waits for his new family to pick him up — or so Stephan thinks.

Once Stephan arrives at Angel Guardian, he is pleasantly surprised by the warmth and kindness extended to him — a vast improvement from his last experiences with the nuns at the orphanages in Italy.

Two nuns, one on each side, take him by the hand and lead him to what appears to be a sort of medical office, where he is given a quick once-over and presented with all new clothing.

His face is gently washed and his hair carefully groomed to perfection. Catching a glimpse of himself in the reflection of a metal cabinet next to the sink, Stephan likes what he sees and, for once, feels a sense of importance with all the fuss being made over him.

Mother Superior, who seems to be totally in charge of the entire production, has Stephan spin around in front of her for her final approval. Clapping in excitement she shouts, "Bravo, Stephan, Bravo!"

Then his family arrives. "Stephan," begins Mother

Superior, "these are your new parents, William and Francesca Wolf." Stephan is coaxed by one of the nuns to extend his little hand in introduction, which he declines as he bows his head, not wishing to make eye contact with these strangers.

Deciding not to force the issue, the Wolfs mumble an excuse about needing to begin their journey back home so as to avoid rush-hour traffic. Mother Superior and the others bid him good luck as they watch a timid Stephan walk independently between his new parents.

Once again, with his worldly belongings in hand, Stephan is escorted out of the adoption home to an awaiting car to travel to yet another destination — a lot of confusion and exhausting travel for this young boy.

Surprisingly, Stephan falls into a deep, peaceful sleep and awakens only when their destination is reached. Still groggy from his nap, he trips out of the car onto his new driveway. The house itself is pleasing to the eye, as are the surrounding homes in his new neighborhood.

William and Francesca gently coax Stephen to follow them up the front walkway lined on either side with colorful, fragrant flowers that form a path to a large porch that wraps around their modest home.

Inside the front door, the trio is greeted by several adult family members awaiting their arrival, one of whom is his new grandmother, Nonna Rosa. She gives Stephan a wink and welcomes him in his native tongue. He briefly allows a smile to form on his face as he exchanges a few pleasantries with Nona Rosa, which makes him feel at ease that at least someone can converse with him and understand his response.

Painfully shy, Stephan chooses to distance himself from any English conversation, which he doesn't understand, anyway — at least not yet.

Bedtime finally arrives, and Stephan is grateful to be out of the spotlight and putting on new cozy pj's. He happily climbs into his very own bed in his very own room. As there are no other children, Stephan must admit to himself that this new family just might be okay, and he promises himself to be more friendly tomorrow. But for now, sleep is the order of the day.

When morning comes, Stephan takes a few moments to orient himself to his new surroundings and remember the happenings of the past few days. His new mother waits patiently for him to adjust, and watches him intently as he slowly begins to move about his new room, exploring what treasures are here for his use and enjoyment.

The irony that his new mother doesn't speak Italian well, even though her own mother, Nonna Rosa, speaks mostly Italian with very few English utterances, causes Stephan to wonder how these people ever understand each other. Then he gets his first lesson on their method of communication as his mother gestures for him to follow her downstairs, which he does with a bit of trepidation.

He sits quietly at the kitchen table while his first American breakfast of freshly squeezed orange juice, bacon and eggs, and whole-wheat toast are prepared for him. An unexpected enthusiastic knocking at the door sends Stephan flying off his chair to the sanctity and shelter of the underside of the kitchen table. Chuckling softly to herself at such a sight, Francesca crosses the kitchen floor to answer the urgent knocking.

"Where is he? Where's the new arrival hiding at?" says a loud male voice resounding through the kitchen.

"Stephan, this is a friend of ours. His name is Shelby, and he is very excited to meet you. Come on out from under the table. It's okay. Honest", his mother reassures.

Not intending to wait a moment longer, Shelby takes matters into his own hands by crouching down under the table, smiling he extends a hand to assist Stephan out of his temporary sanctuary, and lifts him high to the ceiling, laughing and carrying on. Francesca reminds Shelby that Stephan doesn't yet speak or understand any English, but Shelby assures her that won't be a problem between he and the boy. And you know what? ... Shelby is right.

Stephan finds himself giggling and smiling in no time at all, exchanging hand signals with Shelby in a nonverbal communication Stephan finds similar to his past "conversations" with his other friends from the hillside farm. And just like those friends, Shelby doesn't have any hair on his head either!

In the days that follow, Stephan begins to warm up to his new family and is introduced to more and more people every day. In record time, he picks up the English language and is able to articulate his every need, while still retaining a slight Italian accent that everyone finds quite charming.

Much to his parents' dismay, however, Stephan not only excels in learning the English language but all its unsavory slang, as well. To Stephan's delight, the neighborhood children waste no time taking him into their private world of "no adults allowed!" Cool! Very cool!

Stephan is about to attend his first day of school in a few weeks, and his mother takes great pride in dragging him from store to store, looking for just the right outfits for her new pride and joy.

After an exhausting day of shopping, he collapses on the living room couch only to be literally uprooted by his new pal Shelby, who bounds into the house with a surprise package in his hand. Eagerly, Stephan rips open the box to find a new pair of sneakers for school. Sneakers! He had never seen sneakers before coming to America. He was envious of the other children as they ran, jumped, and rode their bikes in comfort. Now he, too, could be just like the other kids.

Stephan's best friend and confidant is a neighbor boy named Tommy O'Malley. How Irish can you get? Tommy is about Stephan's age and has two older brothers — Matthew, age ten, and Brian, age twelve — who take great pleasure in tormenting the younger boys. But Stephan and Tommy, while feigning injustice, participate eagerly in these exchanges and even instigate the majority of the interplay.

Adjusting to school is easy for Stephan. He is exceptionally bright, eager to learn, and gets along quite well with the other students. Surprisingly enough, his previous experiences with the less than desirable foster-home children and the abusive treatment at the orphanage didn't leave Stephan with any permanent emotional scars. His new friends fondly nickname him Steffe, and he likes that.

His parents, while not wishing to change his first name, decide to further Americanize him by changing his name's pronunciation from Ste-phan to Stee-phan, with the spelling remaining the same.

His adopted family's original name was Lupiano and was changed to Wolf when Stephan's adopted father's grandfather came to this country from Italy. Interesting indeed. Stephan can't help but feel Lupo is alive and well and still in his life, even in this far-away land called America.

With fall in full swing, Stephan is continually introduced to new customs and fun seasonal activities. Halloween is fast approaching, and his mother, who has been preparing for this moment for years, its seems, is going all out for Stephan's first Halloween costume.

No amount of protesting can change her course, so he decides it best to ride the wave. What is more American (besides apple pie) than baseball and its heroes? So there he stands, a pintsize, five-year-old replica of the man himself — Joe DiMaggio!

As his mother puts the finishing touches on his costume, Tommy, in full pirate regalia, crashes through the front door with his mother in tow and yells, "Trick or treat! Trick or treat!"

"Why is he saying that, Mom?" asks Stephan.

Realizing she neglected to mention this part of the Halloween tradition, his mother describes the entire process of how to politely partake of the goodies the neighbors have waiting for the ghosts and goblins that roam the streets on this special night.

"Wow! Let's go then!" shouts Stephan. The boys race to the door while their mothers call after them to wait up. But it is wasted breath and energy as the two five-year-olds burst out onto the cold October streets of their transformed suburban neighborhood decorated with jack-o-lanterns and scary Halloween sights and sounds.

Being an American has so many advantages, Stephan muses to himself... Not only do you get to stay out late, but you can ring doorbells and get candy for just saying "Trick or Treat!" I love America!

After an hour or so, the mothers agree it's time to return home, much to the disappointment of Joe DiMaggio and his pirate accomplice. Once in the house, Stephan's mom begins the daunting task of weeding through the candy, which by now he's begun to open and eat all at once.

"Why are you going through the candy?" he asks.

His mother explains there are some people who don't have the right spirit and attitude about children and Halloween, and that sometimes there can be harmful things inside the candy. That's why the moms and dads check it all out before the children can eat the candy. Dumb rule, Stephan thinks, but acquiesces nonetheless.

Suddenly, there is a knock on the door, and Stephan races to answer, prepared to distribute more candy to "trick-or-treaters." To his surprise there stands Tommy and his brothers, Matthew and Brian, dressed up as a football player and a ghost respectively, pleading with Stephan's mother for him to join them for one more go around the neighborhood.

Not wishing to be viewed as a stick in the mud by her son... her son, what a nice ring that has to it, Stephan's mother agrees, but only under the condition that no candy be eaten until she has done her thorough inspection of his treasures. Agreed! Off the four boys go, with the promise to return in an hour.

They no sooner get around the first corner when Matthew and Brian announce they're going to meet some of their friends, and that Tommy and Stephan can continue on their own, but they have to promise not to talk to any strangers, and for heaven's sake don't go home without them or they'll all be in trouble.

They agree to meet at a particular spot in a short while, not that Stephan or Tommy have any idea of the passage of time, but they do understand they have to go home eventually.

Tommy and Stephan soon hook up with another neighbor boy, Daniel, who is wrapped in bandaging from head to toe, with a fake bloodstain on his head. He explains he's an accident-prone mummy. Halloween — what will they think of next? Stephan wonders.

As the evening progresses, the air turns colder and the streets become less and less populated by trick-or-treaters. The boys begin to wonder if enough time has passed, and if they should head back to meet up with Tommy's older brothers. No one takes into consideration that most five-year-olds can't tell time, and even if these three could, none of them was wearing a watch anyway.

Tommy guesstimates they have a little more time, so they collectively agree to travel down one last street in search of the last bit of candy that awaits their confiscation.

Growing weary and disappointed that the street they chose has no porch lights lit, they sit on a curbstone for a while to take inventory of their treasure.

While Daniel and Tommy enthusiastically rummage through their containers filled to the brim with confectionary treats, Stephan gazes longingly skyward. Such a clear, crisp, crystal night sky, with stars twinkling endlessly above.

Tommy stops mid- rummage to ask Stephan "What are you lookin' at?"

"Home," Stephan dreamily replies.

"I thought you said you were from Italy?" Daniel interjects, while continuing his count of confiscated treasures.

"Well, I guess you could say I came from Italy to here … but I came from *there* first." He points to a bright blue-and-white, twinkling star near the horizon.

"How did you get from there to here, then?" Daniel continues casually while his mouth brims with chocolate delights.

"I don't really know. … I just know it's where I'm from," Stephan replies in earnest.

Tommy quietly joins Stephan in his gaze at this amazingly bright star that seems to shout to be noticed with its ceaseless blue-and-white strobing.

In a brotherly gesture, Tommy drapes his arm around Stephan's shoulders and says, "Well, I'm glad you're here with us now, Steffe. Okay, I think it's time we find Matthew and Brian, and go home. I'm cold."

The Shrink

I guess the mastery of my disappearing act in the middle of the night — or perhaps its was my unabashed explanation of where I'd been all night — was the final straw that unnerved my parents enough to think I was compensating on some primal level for being abandoned by my real parents or, at the very least, that I had an unnerving overactive imagination.

I also became quite astute at hiding my true intelligence at school for fear of being ridiculed and cast out from the other kids. I would deliberately flunk tests just so I would be considered to be a normal child struggling with the same academic challenges as everyone else.

At any rate, the end result was that I began having "talks" with a shrink. He was no ordinary shrink, I was to later discover. His name was Dr. Umberto Francisco Ortega, and he specialized in "children like me," whatever that meant.

I still didn't understand what all the fuss was about relative to my drawing, which detailed the inside of a spaceship and my aerial interpretations of the Earth below. These schematics were very clear to me from the nightly visits with my friends, so it was only natural that I would replicate on paper what I had seen firsthand. After all, it was no big deal when I would make renderings of our home or the family pet or some scenic view while amusing myself in the back *seat of the family car while on a road trip. So why this reaction?*

Don't get me wrong, my family loved me very much. I was adored by all my relatives, even though I was categorized as a bit bizarre, and how I often brought my parents to the point of being frantic with some of my stories and wild behavior. They struggled with labeling me either a genius or just plain weird. The latter was the label of choice.

As a result of my nighttime meanderings, my family was the first in our neighborhood to install an alarm system, to monitor my nocturnal whereabouts. Despite this expensive investment and the numerous safety locks placed strategically throughout the house, I still got out. I was often found in my pj's in the early morning hours in a dazed condition, stating most emphatically that I was visiting and traveling around with my "friends" — thus the sessions with the shrink.

I even disappeared for a whole day while vacationing with one of my uncles in Lake George, New York. To this day, I have no recollection of where I was. I just knew that when those kinds of things occurred, I would always return safe and sound.

As if all this weren't enough, being raised Catholic by my adopted American family, I would constantly challenge the church doctrine, much to the horror of my devotedly religious mother and grandmother.

My natural psychic abilities and my assumed blasphemy toward the church all translated to my family to be nothing short of witchcraft. As a matter of fact, Monsignor Monticello was finally called upon to perform a good old-fashioned exorcism to shut me up, but my beliefs never faltered.

To appease my parents and to be more accepted, I agreed to become an alter boy, a position I held for two full years, which ended on my fourteenth birthday.

During all this, I found time to embark on an entrepreneurial career by creating my own Space Club, which consisted of some neighborhood friends and friends I connected with who also attended sessions with Dr. Ortega. No girls allowed though! I say this because there was one chubby little girl whose appointment followed mine who tried her best to join my Space Club, but I wasn't about to break the code of the club or our all-male bond. No way!

As strange as it may sound, I did enjoy my visits with Dr. Ortega, for he truly believed what I told him and showed great interest in the mechanics of it all.

One particular afternoon when I arrived at his office for my usual scheduled appointment, two men in suits met me at the door and rudely asked who I was and why I was there. When I told them I saw Dr. Ortega all the time, they began to ask me all kinds of questions, one right after the other. The whole time this interrogation was going on other men were emptying the file cabinets of their contents and placing these materials into boxes, and hurriedly whisking them out of the building.

When there was a break in the rapid-fire questioning, I found the courage to ask a question myself: "Where is Dr. Ortega?"

The answer not only shocked me, but the manner in which it was delivered went beyond definition. "Oh, he's dead! You can go now."

He's dead? What do you mean, he's dead? Those words hung in the air and echoed in my ears for weeks to come. Surprisingly, my parents were of no help, as they nervously declined to discuss the incident any further.

So my sessions with Dr. Ortega ended as abruptly as they had begun, with no talk about finding another doctor.

One last thing I was told — no I was ordered — not to discuss this with anyone! I also had to stop talking to the other children who had met with Dr. Ortega. End of discussion!

It wasn't until I got to college and reconnected with one of the boys who also saw Dr. Ortega that I found out what really happened to him and the possible implications it had on us all - but I digress.

ॐ

(Flashback)

"Hey there, Steffe! Como esta?" greets Dr. Ortega. Stephan, who by now is comfortable with his weekly sessions with the doctor, responds with a grin as he bursts through the office door to the inner sanctum of the therapy room and plops himself down onto one of the overstuffed chairs. The "hot seat," as Dr. Ortega affectionately calls it.

Stephan has missed a couple sessions with Dr. Ortega because he had been away on spring break from school.

"So, gone anyplace interesting lately?" Dr. Ortega prods in his familiar cavalier style. He reaches to turn on his tape recorder, which is mounted in an inconspicuous location somewhere beneath his desk. Stephan has grown comfortable with this routine. He knows it's part of Dr. Ortega's job but, more importantly, it lends a certain amount of credibility on the good doctor's behalf that he takes Stephan's statements and stories seriously.

"And they're off!" Stephan answers in a somewhat arrogant manner. They both let out a mild chuckle, then Stephan begins, "Actually …"

Intrigued by his lead-in, Dr. Ortega presses Stephan further. Without much encouragement, Stephan recounts his latest episode.

"Over spring break, I spent a week with my Uncle Bill at his cabin on Lake George. Did I ever tell you about him? He's my mom's youngest brother. We get along really great, so he invited me fishing while I was on my vacation. I was psyched! The first couple days were kind of cold and rainy, but the rest of the week the weather got really nice."

Dr. Ortega interrupts Stephan: with "Sounds pretty normal to me so far. Continue." Stephan holds up his hand to gesture "wait, it gets better," causing Dr. Ortega to lean forward in his chair, all ears.

"Wednesday — no, I think it was Thursday — morning

I woke up early. I mean really early. Even Uncle Bill hadn't gotten up yet, and he's up with the birds. I got dressed, grabbed a couple donuts, and a carton of milk, and walked down to the dock that's not far from the front porch of the cabin.

The lake was amazingly still and clear. I could actually see fish swimming below the surface. Without much thought I decided to take advantage of this situation and take the boat out, maybe catch a few fish and surprise my uncle. We always kept the boat ready for fishing, with poles and bait, so I hopped aboard and began rowing."

Stephan stops his narrative and stares off, oblivious to his surroundings and obviously lost in his own thoughts. Dr. Ortega cocks his head then clears his throat in an effort to nudge Stephan out of his self-imposed hypnosis, so he can continue his tale. Stephan, coming back to the reality of the room, adjusts his position in the chair and returns his gaze to Dr. Ortega. and quietly whispers "And that's all I remember".

"What do you mean ... that's all you remember? Did you fall asleep? Did you fall and hit your head and pass out? What do you mean?"

Stephan looks longingly at the doctor as if pleading to understand it himself, but all he can answer is: "I don't know. All I remember is being back in the boat beached on the shore by the dock — not tied up to it, just near it, and it's dark out. My Uncle Bill is shaking me by the shoulders, yelling at me to tell him where I've been all day and why I left without telling him. He was really upset, worried that something bad had happened. Like I might have drowned or something. But I really can't remember ... anything."

Stephan is obviously shaken by recalling this event, yet Dr. Ortega doesn't want this moment to slip away, so he asks Stephan if they can try hypnotic regression. Stephan has done this many times before with Dr. Ortega, and is a willing subject. He, too, wants to get to the bottom of what's happening to him and, most importantly, why.

"Okay, Stephan, let's go over to the recliner and get comfortable. You know the drill." Stephan readies himself as he has done so many times before, then hesitates. "This time I'm a little scared. I don't know exactly why, but I am. I just want you to know that."

Dr. Ortega reaches over to pat Stephan's shoulder. "I will always protect you," he says, "and if you get uncomfortable at any time as we try to figure out what happened that day, I promise to bring you back quickly."

This is exactly why Stephan trusts Dr. Ortega so much. While it's important to get to the bottom of all of this weirdness, Stephan knows Dr. Ortega is his friend and will do anything to keep him safe and minimize any trauma that may result from their findings.

"Ready? ... Let's begin." Dr. Ortega gently begins the process of regressing Stephan by having him close his eyes and breathe deeply. He is to listen only to the sound of the doctor's voice.

Stephan's breathing is slow and steady as he begins to relax, and obediently he shuts out all other sounds. "Relax, relax ... deeper and deeper." He goes into that place where unconscious memory resides. Where the soul keeps it secrets and holds them tightly until demanded to rise to the surface.

Confident that Stephan has reached that place, Dr. Ortega begins the dialogue: "Stephan, I want you to go back a few weeks to your vacation with your Uncle Bill at Lake George. I want you to put yourself right there. See it, smell it, hear the sounds. Are you there, Stephan?"

"Yes," Stephan answers calmly — then:

Dr. O.: *Good, very good. Now I want you to tell me what you see and hear.*

Stephan: *It's really pretty here. It's kind of cold and*

it's raining really hard, but I'm happy. I like being here.

Dr. O.: What are you doing?

Stephan: *Uncle Bill and I are unpacking our gear and putting groceries away. We're talking about hiking in the woods, even though it's raining. I'm thinking, How cool is this? Nobody to tell me I can't go out in the rain because I might get my feet wet and get sick.*

Dr. O.: *Yep, that's very cool, Stephan. Now, I want you to go ahead a bit in time to the day when the rain stopped and you woke up early before your uncle did. Can you do that for me?*

Stephan: *Okay.*

Dr. O.: *You're lying in bed, just opening your eyes. ... Tell me what happens next.*

Stephan: *I look around the room then out the window by my bed and see the sun is up, but it's barely up, so I know it's really early in the morning. I push back the covers and get up and throw on my jeans and a warm flannel shirt I left on the floor last night. I probably should put on a clean shirt, but I don't care.*

Dr. Ortega smiles and stifles a snicker as he thinks how Stephan can seem so normal at times. Just a typical preteen boy. But he quickly pulls himself back to the task at hand and asks Stephan to keep going and tell him what happens next.

Stephan: *I'm out in the living room, and I see that Uncle Bill's bedroom door is closed. Guess he's still sleeping. Boy, this is a first. Me waking up before him! I'm hungry. I see a box of donuts on the counter and grab two of the white, sugar-coated ones. I like those best. I open the refrigerator and take out a small carton of milk to wash it all down with. I'm looking out the front picture window at the lake and thinking, I want to go outside. So I do.*

Dr. Ortega decides to move the process along a bit faster and asks:
Stephan place yourself down by the dock and describe how you are feeling and what you're thinking.

Stephan: *I feel great. I'm not hungry anymore. I'm looking at how clear the water is. I can see fish! Lot's of fish. Big ones! Boy, I want to go out and catch some and bring them back before Uncle Bill even knows I'm gone. It's warming up. The sun feels good. I don't think I need a jacket. The boat is tied to the dock, with fishing poles and a can of live worms. Perfect! I'm going out to fish.*

Dr. O.: *Tell me what you're thinking now. Are you afraid to go out by yourself?*

Stephan: *No. It's not a big lake. I can row out a little ways and cast my line and still see the cabin. It's not far. I'm okay.*

Dr O.: *All right. Stephan, where are you now and what are you doing?*

Stephan: *I'm about a hundred yards out. I can still see the cabin, and there's no wind, so I'm not drifting or anything. I'm looking through the can of worms to pick out a couple lively ones. Found one! Great! I'm putting it on the hook and casting it over the water. This is cool. This is very cool ... wait! Wait a minute ... it's all black! It's all black! I can't see! I can't see! What's that noise?*

Dr. O.: *Okay, Stephan. I want you to relax and breathe slowly and deeply for me. You're all right. I'm here with you. Just relax ... relax.*

Stephan obediently begins taking slow breaths in and out as he is told. Dr. Ortega reaches for Stephan's wrist and confirms his pulse is at a normal rhythm.

Dr. O.: *Good, Stephan. Just relax. You all right to continue?*

Stephan: *Yeah ... sure.*

Dr. O.: *Okay then. Have you ever experienced this before?*

Stephan: *Actually, yeah. But never this dark and never for this long. Guess it kind of freaked me out.*

Dr. O.: *What does the blackness and the noise mean?*

Stephan: *It means they're coming. Whenever they come, it gets dark like this. But first, there's always a humming sound.*

Dr. O.: *Who's coming, Stephan?*

Stephan: *They're coming ... my friends are coming ... Lupo is coming!*

Dr. Ortega has regressed Stephan many times before, but this time he notices a different pattern in the boy's reaction to the regressive memory event. He is keenly aware that even Stephan, with his high level of paranormal experience, is having difficulty wrapping sense around this particular event, so Dr. Ortega must proceed ever so carefully, so as not to upset Stephan or, even worse, lose Stephan in a posttraumatic episode.

> Dr. O.: Before we continue, I want you know I'm right here with you and that I'll stay right with you. You have nothing to fear. I want you to tell me exactly, in as much detail as possible, all that is happening — who you are with and what you are witnessing. I won't ask any questions for now. You just talk. But I do want you to tell me if you begin to feel uncomfortable. I promise I'll bring you out any time you ask. Quickly. Okay, Stephan? Go ahead. Tell me what's happening.

> Stephan: It's getting lighter now. I feel better. I see lots of light. Really bright ... white, white, white, no ... now there are lots of colors. Like a rainbow, only it's swirling around me like I'm in some kind of tunnel. Colors everywhere!
> Wait! I see something. Looks like ... oh, I see ... it's them! Guess they found a new way to visit me. There are three of them. We're talking, but there's no sound. I hear them, but their lips aren't moving. We walk without using our feet ... kind of floating. They're taking me through a series of tunnels ... hallways ... I can't really describe — blurry, traveling really fast through them.
> Two of them are no longer here. Don't know where they went. It's is just me and the third one. He feels more familiar to me. Somehow, I feel we've done this many times before, just not in this way.
> He leads me to a door I float through. I mean — I don't open it — I just go through it. On the other side are many others. Five, six, no ... seven beings surrounded by more bright light. I mean it's REALLY bright, but my eyes don't hurt. They look like the others, only bigger.
> The size of their heads and the dark coverings over their eyes freak me out. Sort of like sunglasses, but without the earpieces. I don't see any ears anyway.
> They welcome me and speak of how long it's been since I've been with them. Then one moves closer and begins to ask me

questions. I think this one's in charge.

I'm giving them a lot of information, but for some reason I can't remember exactly what I'm telling them. It's like I'm observing all this and not really part of it.

Now they're showing me some TV-like screens with charts with longitudes and latitudes. It looks like maps of the Earth.

I'm feeling a sudden intense surge of energy in my head. At first it's just like a humming, a buzzing that's getting louder and louder. Wait a minute ... it's starting to hurt ... I'm putting my hands over my ears to muffle the sound, but it doesn't help. I'm looking at them, pleading for them to stop this noise in my head, but they just continue to watch me.

Stop! Stop it! It hurts! Why aren't they helping? I feel like my head's going to explode. Help! Stop it! God ... help me!"

Stephan is thrashing about, screaming for the pain to stop.

Dr. O.: *Stephan, Stephan, it's all right. I'll bring you back now. You don't have to stay there. Just listen to my voice. You will only hear my voice. Stephan, can you hear me?*

Struggling to contain his pain, Stephan, eyes still closed, grips both ears as he writhes in agony, pleading over and over to stop the session.

Dr. O.: *Stephan, I'm right here with you. Together we're going to get you out of there. I want you to hear only my voice. Stephan, all is well. You are safe; you are in control of your body and mind. You can come back right now! You only have to focus on my voice and follow it back into my office. Breathe, Stephan, BREATHE!*

Dr. Ortega is desperate to bring Stephan back unharmed, yet he knows he must do this slowly and deliberately. He continues his instructions and is relieved when he finally sees the telltale signs of Stephan's return.

Stephan's breathing grows less labored, and he regains a more normal rhythmic pattern. His face begins to relax and he no longer winces in pain.

Once confident that Stephan has fully returned to this reality, Dr. Ortega takes a moment to catch his own breath before instructing Stephan to open his eyes.

Stephan, exhausted from the mental journey, wipes his moist eyes with both hands as he slowly sits up from his reclined position and quips solemnly, "Wow! How was that, Doc?"

Dr. Ortega can only respond with wonderment of how surreal and unabashedly frightening this kind of experience must be for a young person. As an adult professional who thought he had seen and heard it all, he discovers that he was scared out of his own wits at what must have really gone on for Stephan, at least in his mind.

Above all, Dr. Ortega knows he must continue working with Stephan to uncover why he has been chosen and what he has been chosen to do.

Pouring Stephan a glass of water, Dr. Ortega comforts him as best he can and cautions him to not discuss this session with anyone. "We've just begun getting into some important new territory with this one, Stephan. Let's keep this between us until we can make some sense of it all. Agreed?"

With little more than a few exchanged words, Stephan and Dr. Ortega part company, with mumblings of ...See you next week.

After escorting Stephan out of his office, Dr. Ortega locks the door behind him as he has no other scheduled appointments for the day. He plops himself heavily upon the recliner reserved for his clients' sessions and tries to regain some semblance of professional objectivity to what he's just witnessed. Working with these extraordinary children has proven to be an experience that even he couldn't have possibly prepared for.

All of Dr. Ortega's young patients have unusual stories to share, but he has become acutely aware that Stephan along with two other children go far beyond the others in their intense experiences and aptitudes.

Dr. Ortega rises from the recliner and moves to his file cabinet, where he shuffles through its contents until he reaches the files of the two other children, Elizabeth and Nathan, who exhibit the same type of paranormal episodes as Stephan.

Moving slowly back to his desk, he opens the files and rereads excerpts from the other two children's sessions, searching for a common denominator that might link these three patients together.

Elizabeth is about the same age as Stephan, and Dr. Ortega smiles a bit as he pores over his side notes about how she compensates emotionally with her ordeals through overeating. Not an uncommon tool for children who are stressed and need to find comfort in whatever way they can.

Dr. Ortega then turns his attention to the other file. Nathan is a little older than Stephan and Elizabeth. Beyond the age difference, the doctor makes mental note of Nathan's odd physical appearance compared to the other two.

Nathan is quite tall and slender for his age, and exhibits a strange detachment from his environment. He displays almost robotic movements, along with eyes that don't show a lot of connection to Dr. Ortega or the world around him. He speaks in a monotone with little to no inflection to his voice, with the exception of when Dr. Ortega implements a regression therapy session. Then, and only then, does Nathan break out of his protective cocoon and show any type of real emotion.

Puzzling, indeed, to see three different children whose reactions to their extraordinary experiences are as remote from one another as they could possibly be, and yet there is a connection among them. Dr. Ortega is almost sure of it now.

He determines he must place the majority of his professional focus on these three specific children if he is to ever get to the bottom of this amazing mystery.

In his solitude, Dr. Ortega ponders the depth of what this all means in terms of reality. Reality. Is there such a thing? Sure, but there is never just one true reality. There are many, and these three children are displaying their abilities to cross over from one reality to another as willing guinea pigs on behalf of whom? And for what purpose?

When Dr. Ortega was first approached by a branch of the C.I.A. and wooed to leave his comfortable general practice of child psychology to specialize in working with children exhibiting paranormal prowess, he thought, Sure, why not? Could be an intriguing experience with groundbreaking results — not to mention a welcome professional challenge.

Little did he realize the enormity of the task at hand and, more importantly, the impact these children would have on him, not only as a professional but as a human being on this planet, in this galaxy, in this universe!

Now, as he sits dumbfounded by his latest session with Stephan and tries to connect the dots between Nathan and Elizabeth, he begins to grasp the enormity of the situation and begins to wonder if these children could possibly be in any danger — and not just from the aliens they purport to be in contact with.

He has no sooner finished that thought when he hears a noise that seems to be coming from his outer office. As he slowly rises from his desk to investigate, he searches his memory ... didn't I already lock the front door?

He opens the door from his private office to the waiting room and is shocked to see two tall, dark figures standing side by side before him, approaching without hesitation or saying a word.

Dr. Ortega demands: "Who are you?" but the figures

keep coming, forcing him to instinctively back all the way into his private office, stopping only because he is met with the front of his desk and can go no farther.

His heart races wildly as he senses what is to come. The only sound besides the pounding of his heart is a trembling whispered prayer emitting from his lips as he utters his final plea.

Back On The Farm

O*kay, so what kid wouldn't love to visit his aunt and uncle and favorite cousin, Paul, on their farm in Idaho for two weeks during summer vacation?*

It was my thirteenth birthday. My coming of age. Knowing how much I missed hanging out with my cousin Paul, my parents thought they'd surprise me with this special gift. You know that old expression, "You can take the boy out of the country ..."

Oh, I adapted to living in the suburbs just fine and learned how to be an all-American boy in record time. But my heart always returned to those early recollections and happiest memories of my days with my first foster family on their farm high atop the hillside in Italy.

Farm life to me always represented a special connection to the earth and to nature and, most especially, those visits with my "special" friends — and Lupo.

What a blast I had with Paul and his rowdy band of friends. Farm life for teenage boys with raging hormones can be duller than watching paint dry. But Paul and his buddies always seemed to make the best of it and pushed the edge of the envelope just enough to stay out of any serious trouble.

Emerging into teenagehood held the promise of exciting changes and endless possibilities. Little did I know exactly how much my life was about to change, once again, in a way that even I couldn't have seen coming.

It was a typical sultry August day with the threat of impending summer thunderstorms off in the distance. Larry, one of the band of merry men, had liberated a pack of Winston cigarettes from his older brother's shirt pocket, along with several back issues of Playboy he hoped his father wouldn't miss for very long.

Sitting atop the ranch rail fence that bordered Paul's property with his neighbor's there we all sat, smoking, sipping Cokes, and talking about, — what else? — girls and how can we get their attention. Just five guys goofing off on a lazy Thursday in August in a wheatfield in Idaho.

To spice things up a bit, we challenged each other to a race through the cornfields and wheat fields to see who could run the fastest and sustain running the longest, in spite of our newly developed cigarette coughs. Nasty habit!

Whooping and hollering as we ran unencumbered through the fields was exhilarating, and we felt like fearless Masters of the Universe. That is, until we stumbled onto something that changed our lives forever — or at least mine.

I can't remember who exactly made the discovery first, but suddenly we all came to a screeching halt and surveyed the surrounding terrain in awe of what appeared to be one of those crop circles. Now we had heard of them, of course, and thought they were a bunch of hooey.

Now, here we were right smack dab in the middle of that hooey, frozen solid to the spots where we stood.

A couple of the guys stuttered some type of reasonable explanation for what or who could have done this, but their reasoning quickly fell apart as they crouched to inspect the crushed plants under our feet.

It didn't take long before one by one, or maybe two by two, the guys began to peel off in haste, shouting such nonsense as "Well, g-g-gotta go ... my p-p-arents will be looking for me.... D-d-dinner's about ready ... see ya later! ..." And off they all ran, with *the exception of Paul and me.*

For some unknown reason, Paul hesitated along with me. Maybe he wanted to see what I would do first, before he surrendered to the fight or flight syndrome.

Right from my first days in America, Paul was the one I confided in the most when others wouldn't listen or allow me to talk about my "other life" — how I knew things and how I believed I came from another place, a place called Sirius.

Even as a young boy, Paul humored my ramblings and let me speak about it all, never judging, just listening. Oh, once in a while he would say something like "Wow, that's really far out there, Steffe," and occasionally he'd ask a question or two. But for the most part, Paul accepted this part of who I was or, at least, who I thought I was. I was always grateful for his unconditional acceptance of me.

Both of us now silent, I began to walk even deeper into the center of the circle. Paul became increasingly uneasy and suggested maybe we, too, should head back home, as the other boys had done.

Without answering, I walked even deeper into the circle.

Paul couldn't contain his anxiety any longer and finally declared that he was leaving and that I could stay if I wanted to. Like a dog with its tail between its legs, Paul hurried off, all the while mumbling some inaudible warnings to me. So there I stood all by myself. Waiting. Listening.

ॐ

(Flashback)

Standing inside the massive circle of wheat detailed with artistic swirls and intricate weaves, Stephan, now totally transfixed upon this discovery, begins to feel a low vibration, a pulsing barely felt or heard, but nonetheless there.

As he strains his ears to identify the source of this sound, the vibration becomes more pronounced and begins to take on a harmonic resonance that can only be likened to a symphony tuning up before a performance. "Hum-m-m-m, hum-m-m-m."

Slowly he begins to turn, first in one direction, then in the other, trying to identify the etiology of the sound as its volume increases. "Oh-m-m-m-m-, OH-M-m-m, OH-M-M-m, OH-M-M-M!"

There's a strange familiarity to this humming. Stephan cocks his head all the while turning, listening, and then turning again. "OH-M-M-M, OH-M-M-M, OH-M-M-M!"

It seems to be coming from everywhere now! Above him, below him, from the right, from the left, even from inside of him! Louder and louder. "OH-M-M-M ... OH-M-M-M-M ... OH-M-M-M-M!"

His concentration is momentarily broken by a large flock of geese honking in flight formation above him. When the geese reach the epicenter of the crop circle, they chaotically disburse in every direction, squawking and screeching as they pass overhead as if some invisible force field has disrupted their flight path.

Then he feels it! An amazing, powerful, vibrating energy so strong that every fiber of his being pulsates in rapture with this enormous harmonic sound. "OH-M-M-M-M ... OH-M-M-M-M ... OH-M-M-M-M!"

No longer in control of his body, he feels his arms rise from his sides, palms up, face tilted to the sky, eyes gently closed so he may relish each sound, each vibration. "OH-M-M-M-M ... OH-M-M-M-M ... OH-M-M-M-M!"

Totally mesmerized, he begins a slow spin around and around like a dancer performing choreographic movements to the harmonies that now completely envelop him. "OH-M-M-M-M-M ... OH-M-M-M-M-M ... OH-M-M-M-M-M!"

Totally lost in his reverie, he ignores the rustling sounds emulating from the undisturbed wheat that surrounds the circle. So absorbed in ecstasy, he will not be distracted from this moment. "OH-M-M-M-M-M ... OH-M-M-M-M-M ... OH-M-M-M-M-M!"

As if on cue, they emerge from the thick magical blades of the wheat field's perimeter. First one, then two, then a half-dozen stealthful wolves surround Stephan. Licking at his legs, bumping their heads to his body in a low posture denoting their submissive greeting reserved for only the highest creature in the animal kingdom — the alpha male — Lupo!

"OH-M-M-M-M-M-M ... OH-M-M-M-M-M ... OH-M-M-M," blackness, then silence.

Stephan awakens bewildered, his body outstretched as he lies face up in the center of the crop circle floor. He is all alone in complete, deafening silence. Had he somehow fallen asleep? Was it all a dream? Is he still dreaming? *NO!* He knows better.

Even though it's been some time since he has allowed himself to be receptive to visits from his *friends*, due to peer pressure and that of his parents, Stephan smiles with the assuredness that this was anything *but* a dream.

Lupo has once again reactivated the wisdom of the Elders to this now-thirteen-year-old receiver, whose mission is clearer than ever before, a mission he will obey without question.

Stephan will not talk of this day to anyone, not even to his closest confidant, Paul. For he knows this is way beyond Paul's benevolent understanding. He also knows he cannot divulge, at least not yet, the honorary task assigned to him.

Recalling his recent studies in school of the Hopi Indian tribe, now — more than ever — he understands their prophecy: *"We are the ones we've been waiting for."*

Soon, he tells himself, soon they'll all know of this. For now, Stephan will hold tight to his mission.

The Other E.T.

After graduating from high school, I set my sights on a career in the legal field. I had applied to several excellent law schools and was pleased to have been accepted to George Washington University. Although it wasn't my first choice, it certainly held its own reputation for graduates being placed in solid, well-established law firms. That was good enough for me.

So at the end of a crazy summer of partying and saying goodbye to my family and my closest friends, I once again packed up most of my earthly belongings, at least those I could fit into my 1972 Chevy Camaro that my Uncle Bill gifted to me, and drove to Washington, D.C., and my new life at George Washington University.

While I purposely wasn't the best student in the world, I at least held my grade average and earned enough extra credits to obtain a partial scholarship. Between my parents' remortgaging the house and the generous contributions from my aunt and uncle on my father's side who had no children of their own, I was able to afford to attend such a prestigious school.

I was the "great white hope" in my family, as they were mostly working-class people who earned an honest living at a variety of crafts. My parents were literally betting all their money on me and my future as an attorney.

I'll never forget my father's tearful speech as he cornered me at my going-away party. Admittedly, he had imbibed in one too many Rum and Cokes while my mother played the perfect hostess in our small but well-appointed patio ideal for just such a gathering. But the words he spoke stopped me dead in my tracks as he looked me straight in the eye and told me of how at first he wasn't so sure about adopting a child, but wanted to make my mother happy.

Before I could get my feathers ruffled, he continued to recount my early struggles as a "different kind of kid" who wasn't always understood, but was always loved and cherished beyond words.

He acknowledged my academic acumen in certain subject matters — such as math, science, and languages — and how he never dreamed I would someday choose to focus on becoming an attorney, which by his family's standards was right up there with becoming President of the United States. A proud father, indeed.

Seeing that his emotions were on the verge of running amuck, I quickly took control of the conversation by reminding him of some ridiculous stunt I had pulled one day at high school that resulted in my getting an inside suspension, which basically meant I could go to school but not to class. Go figure.

Now, while this type of behavior would bring most parents to their knees asking God what they had done wrong to have raised such a child, my father found great humor in my shenanigans, at least at this level. My sleepwalking, psychic premonitions, and disappearing acts were another matter entirely. Those he never understood, and I guess what ultimately happened was that he chose to ignore them altogether, which translated to him as their never having happened in the first place. Problem solved.

I was deeply touched by his words and that he took the initiative to send me out into the world knowing I am deeply loved. It meant a lot to me, as I usually felt so different from most of my adopted family. For that matter, from the rest of humanity!

My first week at George Washington University was just as you would expect a first week at a new school away from home to be. Chaotic, to say the least, but totally exhilarating, to say the most.

Here you have young men and women, most of whom are experiencing true freedom for the first time in their young lives, allowed to come and go as they please. Very empowering and confusing all at the same time. I, on the other hand, enjoyed the lack of structure and found great comfort in winging it.

Once I located my dormitory building and my room, I began the unmitigated chore of unloading my car, which, by the way, was parked in a lot so far from my room that I seriously considered paying one of the other students to drive me back and forth. Of course, I later learned there was a parking lot much closer to my new living quarters, but the upperclassmen weren't about to share that valuable piece of information with a lowly freshman. NO WAY!

Continuing with my lucky streak, my roommate was a quiet and unassuming guy from the Midwest, whose only focus was on his studies and sleeping. Actually, in hindsight, Jeffrey was probably the only roommate who would have worked for me at that stage in my life, as I was struggling to keep my "other" talents hidden, at least for now.

I had become quite adept at explaining how I would be found in my underwear or, on certain occasions, al naturale, standing outside my room or, better yet, outside the dorm building on my return trip from one of my visitations. The one good thing about college life is that anything and everything is expected, and usually there are no questions asked. Just a rolling of the eyes or a shaking of the head, accompanied by muffled snickering. Thank you, God!

My classes were mainstream pre-law with an occasional elective that was like a breath of fresh air. One such class was The Study of Psychological Phenomenon, which was right up my alley. Here the discussions and research focused on the paranormal, such as poltergeists, ghosts, possession, UFOs and, of course, E.T.'s.

As you can imagine, this was a no-brainer for me, and my professor found me fascinating as I went on with my postulations on space travel and life on other planets. I'd be willing to bet he thought I was either a genius or some egghead whose imagination was enhanced by one of many available mind-altering substances that could be readily found on campus. At any rate, he enjoyed my banter and the thought-provoking elements I brought to class. If he only knew ...

But it wasn't all business, as I was soon to discover. A late registrant to the class, Elizabeth Tanner joined our motley crew and, I must say, added greatly to the climate of the surroundings.

Appearing somewhat aloof at first, she had a terrific sense of humor and challenged Professor Nordstar daily with her unprecedented line of questioning that had us all waiting with bated breath to see how she would unravel his demeanor, yet once again.

It seemed like she knew something nobody else did, and she exhibited great joy in keeping her secret. I know this sounds corny, but there was something familiar about her.

She was an attractive, petite brunette with piercing crystal blue eyes — a most unusual color combination as her eyes were the most brilliant blue I had ever seen. The kind of blue one would associate with a towheaded blonde, not someone with her dark coloring.

As time went on, Liz, as she liked to be called, and I became very close and enjoyed sharing some pretty way-out theories on what is unseen by most. But there was one particular event that happened between us that became a defining moment in both our lives.

Liz and I wanted to take advantage of a day off from our studies, so we decided to make a day of it and head off campus to enjoy the sights. Our first stop was the Washington National Zoo.

As we walked about, taking in all the animal exhibits, we found ourselves stopped directly in front of the wolf enclosure. We both became silent as we observed these beautiful animals, each in our own thoughts.

I remember clearly that I was in one of my "exchange" modes with an alpha male wolf that sat directly in front of me, with the safety of the glass partition between us.

This was a familiar scenario for me, as I have been communicating with Lupo since I was a young boy. Unbeknownst to me, Liz was doing exactly the same thing.

She was the one who finally broke the silence by making a comment about how distressed this alpha male was in his captivity. I, on the other hand, was shocked to hear her confirm the exact same information this Lupo had just shared with me!

Now, I'm not talking about a general assumption one would make that an animal held in captivity is unhappy. I'm talking about a verbatim recounting of what this alpha male shared with me just moments before!

This marked the beginning of an amazing discovery that would forever alter the course of Liz's and my individual journeys.

ॐ

(Flashback)

"What? You think you're the only one who can hear them? It's about time you figured out who you're dealing with, Preppy," Liz teases.

Stephan stands in silent amazement as she arrogantly turns on her heels and heads toward another exhibit. When he finally regains his composure, he calls after her, "Whoa, wait a minute! Hold on a second!"

When he catches up to her, he reaches for her arm and spins her around, all the while searching her eyes for more explanation. Liz giggles and pulls her arm away stating, "I was wondering how long it would take you to figure it out."

Still confused, Stephan asks if they can sit a minute while he puts it all into focus. Liz complies, and as they sit on a nearby bench, Stephan wipes off the beads of sweat that have formed on his forehead. Seeing that he's having difficulty formulating the words he wants to speak, Liz decides to help him out. She takes a deep breath and begins her explanation.

"I guess I should start by apologizing for having some fun at your expense. Guess it's something I enjoy doing. I've had to create some jokes along the way, so I won't go mad myself."

Liz can tell her opening statement has not helped Stephan's confusion, so she continues in earnest, "Do you remember the feeling you had when we first met? That *I've met you before* thing that's hard to explain? Well, we did meet before, but it was many years ago, when we were both pretty young." She continues, "Like you, I have always been *different*. I, *too*, know things, see things.

"I was a patient of Dr. Ortega's, just like you, and for the exact same reasons you talked with him. I, also, was taken by aliens, E.T.'s — whatever you want to call them — and shown things I couldn't explain to anyone. They all thought I was nuts!"

By now Stephan's confusion has turned to complete focus on the words Liz is speaking. The roaring in his ears has stopped, and he is once again able to fully concentrate on and begin to comprehend what she is telling him.

"You were there, too?" he whispers when he finally finds his voice.

"Yes, and I remember you sitting in the waiting room. You always were before my appointments, Friday afternoons at four."

He rapidly blinks his eyes as he tries to remember those days, and finally raises his eyebrows as clarity sweeps over him. "Yes!" Stephan shouts, "Yes, I remember a chubby little girl sitting in the waiting room who was always eating a large bag of potato chips when I would come out of Dr. Ortega's office."

"Hey, wait a minute," she chimes in, "I was a chubby little girl because I found my only solace in food. Kind of a nervous eating thing. Anyway, I'm over that now", Liz says with pride as she runs her hands demurely down her curvaceous yet athletic form.

Stephan, with a million questions racing through his

mind, blurts out some sort of feeble acknowledgement of her current more desirable appearance. But his real thoughts are still formulating.

"Answer me this," he continues. "With all our conversations, how is it I never knew you were from the same town I grew up in? Dr. Ortega was supposed to be one of only a few doctors specializing in 'kids like us.' But, more importantly, I'm blown away by what are the odds that you and I would attend the same college, let alone become friends. Help me out here!" he pleads.

In an effort to calm Stephan, Liz gently places her hand over his before she speaks. "Well, I wasn't exactly from your town. Actually, I lived in a town kind of far away. Over fifty miles away, to be exact. My parents, who are quite comfortable financially and still hold a high profile in our community, couldn't risk the scandal of a child of theirs seeing a shrink, let alone that their child believes she's the recipient of frequent alien abductions by them."

"Besides, as you said, Dr. Ortega was the only one in his field close enough to see me on a regular basis. Believe me, if he hadn't been so close, my parents would have shipped me off in a New York minute to some boarding school or somewhere else less obvious."

Beginning to accept Liz's story, Stephan still has difficulty trying to figure out the synchronicity of their scholastic endeavors.

For the first time, Liz hesitates before she speaks. Shifting her body to the edge of the bench, she leans into him, closer than a piece of paper or a coat of wax would be, as the saying goes.

Her eyes completely fix upon Stephan's, she places both her hands on his, and starts slowly, "When I was younger, I mean *really* younger, I ran away. At least, that's what they told me I did. There's a small patch of woods behind the house where I grew up, and for the most part I never wanted to go in there because my older brother and sister would terrorize me with stories of monsters and other creepy things in the woods.

"But one night, for whatever reason, I found myself smack dab in the middle of the woods, in my pajamas no less! I couldn't have been any older than three! I sat looking around in the dark waiting … for what? I didn't know. Then this wolf appeared and walked right up beside me and sat down."

"The funny thing is I don't remember feeling scared at all. I didn't touch the wolf; at least, I don't think I did. I just stared into his big yellow eyes. I must have fallen asleep at some point because the next thing I remember was waking up still in the woods, but it was daylight, and I was by myself, with no sign of the wolf. I wondered if I'd been sleepwalking or dreaming, but I truly believed it all happened."

Without regard to Stephan's reaction, she continues: "From that moment on, I just knew I had something I must do."

"As I got older, my studies and research became almost obsessive when it came to UFOs, alien abductions, and other similar phenomena. But in answer to your question as to why I chose this particular school — I don't have an answer, Stef. … I really don't."

Stephan, still locked silently in full attention to Liz, finally looks down before he speaks. "I do, at least I *think* I do."

He clears his throat. "It's no coincidence we came together at this time in our lives. I had a similar experience at a very young age, an encounter with a wolf. Only I call him Lupo — Italian for 'wolf.'

"When I was three, I lived with a foster family on a farm in the hills of Italy, and I ran off into the night to find Lupo. As amazing as it sounds, I wasn't afraid either; in fact, I recall purposely going out to look for him."

"I, also knew some things I couldn't possibly have

known or shared with anyone, for that matter, because I would have most certainly been sent away."

Now, it's Liz who sits speechless as Stephan recounts his parallel experience.

Trembling, Stephan adds, "I'm going to step way out on this very shaky limb and tell you what I think — no, what I *believe* to be so. You and I, and God knows how many others, have been 'chosen' to do something extraordinary. Alone, who knows how far we'd get? Together, I think we're unstoppable. Remember what the bible says: "Whenever two or more of you are gathered in his name …"

I suppose under ordinary circumstances Stephan's revelations would be met with some measure of resistance pressing him for further explanation as to what the heck he means. But these are anything but ordinary circumstances. In fact, there is nothing ordinary about either Liz or Stephan.

Liz finally breaks the long silent pause, nodding her head in complete affirmation as she utters, "… and so it is!"

With that, Stephan and Liz rise up off the bench in unison, still clutching each other's hand as Stephan gestures the universal "After you."

As they walk together, trancelike, toward the zoo exit, they find it's no longer necessary to speak. For they are now bonded in thought and purpose.

In their hearts they know they are gearing up for another kind of rocket ride. The rocket ride of their lives!

Nathan

While I was attending sessions with Dr. Ortega, there was another boy that I would occasionally run into. His name was Nathan and he was really strange. By that, I mean he seemed almost disconnected from what was going on around him.

Whenever I would try to start up some small talk with him, he would vacantly stare back at me as if he were translating what I was saying into his own language, whatever that was.

After a while I stopped trying to have conversations with him, and we would just ignore each other whenever we found ourselves in the same room.

At any rate, imagine my surprise to find Nathan in one of my elective classes — The Study of Psychological Phenomenon — at George Washington University. Nathan was a bit older than I, but as far as elective classes go, any student may attend. Funny how some things never change, and Nathan proved that theory to be an exact science. He was just as distant, uncommunicative, and even more strange, if that was possible.

The dichotomy about it all was his uncanny coincidental run-ins with either me or Elizabeth (Liz) Tanner. Liz and I would often comment: "Okay, isn't it about time for that weirdo to show?" — and sure enough there he'd be, sitting in some corner either reading or observing. Observing what? you ask. Who knew!

LUPO: CONVERSATIONS WITH AN E.T.

It was like he was taking notes or something on human behavior as he clearly lacked any semblance of that himself. And yet, I must admit that I found him fascinating in an Alfred Hitchcock sort of way. You know what I mean? The guy totally creeped me out, and yet I found myself riveted to his odd physicality and the way he would cock his head from one side to the other as if trying to assimilate what he was observing.

Liz told me that she had a very in-depth conversation with Nathan one day after class and that she found him brilliant, albeit strange. She commented on the blankness in his eyes and how even though she knew he was looking at her, she almost felt like there was nothing and no one behind those dark ebony eyes.

She admitted a strange attraction to him and found that while she consciously would try to avoid him at all costs, unconsciously she felt compelled to engage in rather intense dialogue with him postulating the possibilities of life on other planets and alien beings among us. Pretty much the kind of stuff she and I would discuss at great length, but somehow with Nathan it took on a more deliberate serious tone.

Liz and I would often chuckle to ourselves about how Nathan reminded us of an alien himself, with his lack of emotion and robotic movements seeming not of this earth. In hindsight, one might compare him to the emotionless Mr. Spock of the hit TV series Star Trek. Great analogy.

So you can imagine my shock when one day Nathan sought me out, wanting to know if I'd meet him for a bite to eat.

I searched desperately for a clever reason to decline but came up dry, so I agreed to meet him at a local pub just off campus at seven that night.

In an effort to ease my discomfort and since he and Liz already knew each other, I asked Nathan if he'd have a problem with Liz joining us. To my surprise, he responded with a resounding "Yes!" He would prefer we meet alone. No other excuses or explanations.

Okay! So I guess it would be just Nathan and me. What could he possibly want to talk about? The answer would soon be made clear. Very clear.

ॐ

(Flashback)

As Stephan finishes preparing a mock brief for tomorrow's midterm exam in criminal law, he finds himself getting a bit anxious about his scheduled meeting with Nathan. He can't quite put his finger on why he's uncomfortable, just that he would feel a lot better if Liz were permitted to join them.

But it is not to be. So Stephan gulps down the last of his now-warm Coke and quickly checks his reflection in the silver metal lamp on his desk. He flies out of his dorm room, grabbing his light jacket that hangs disheveled on the doorknob. Once in his car, Stephan reaches for the radio to drown out the myriad of anxious questions he has about this impending encounter.

Arriving a few minutes earlier than scheduled, Stephan shuts off his car and sits in silence, contemplating the posture he will present to Nathan, so his true feelings will not be evident.

Taking one last calming deep breath, he boldly steps out of his car and walks to the entrance of the pub, only to find Nathan walking in at exactly the same moment. Coincidence? Perhaps.

With little verbal acknowledgement, Nathan indicates to Stephan to move forward, as the unlikely duo mutually agree to sit in a booth that is located in a far corner of the pub. It is at this moment that Stephan feels like a pawn in some kind of spy movie or some illegal covert operation. He muffles a slight giggle, no doubt brought about by his ever-growing nervousness.

Nathan breaks the uncomfortable silence by asking

Stephan if he would like to order some food first. Stephan nods in agreement and summons the waitress over to take their orders. Once that's out of the way, Stephan decides to takes charge and asks, "Okay, Nathan ... what's this all about?"

Nathan begins, "I had a discussion with your friend Elizabeth — and I believe you like to call her Liz — a few discussions, actually, that I found quite intriguing. She's a very bright young woman, don't you agree?" He states in a flat monotone voice.

Stephan studies Nathan's body language, which reveals nothing more than a cool, detached body sitting in front of him while his mouth formulates understandable language. Weird, very weird.

Nathan continues despite Stephan's lack of response to his statement about Liz. "Liz and I spoke of many things. In particular, we conversed at length about the possibility — no, let me correct that — the probability of life on other planets, both in and outside our galaxy."

"I, for one, feel no need to explore this perplexity any further; nonetheless, I find the contrasting theories and objections by the human race on this subject to be so ... absolutely fascinating." Nathan concludes with no hint of excitement or emotion.

He goes on, "How do you respond to this ongoing investigation of other life forms?"

Stephan, still unsure what Nathan is leading to, answers briefly, "Well, I too, am intrigued by the subject matter and like to consider all things possible. Forgive me for pursuing the issue Nathan, but again, what's this got to do with me?I'm sure you didn't ask me here to meet you in some dark corner of a restaurant just to formulate or expand upon our personal theories on the status of possible galactic inhabitants, did you?", Stephan snips back.

Never losing his cool demeanor, Nathan replies, "Well,

you're not totally wrong there. As a matter of fact, I suppose I do wish to expand this 'intrigue,' as you call it, but not in the way you may be anticipating. Let me clarify."

Stephan quips back a flat" Please do."

"I find our paths have crossed more than once. Were you aware that I, too, was a patient of Dr. Ortega's when I was a young boy, such as you?"

By this time Stephan is mesmerized and feeling a bit dizzy at this revelation. "Go on ..."

"Well, my reasons for seeing Dr. Ortega were similar to yours, I would assume however, there were some differences. I also believe Elizabeth's 'talents,' if you will, were a bit of a different nature as well."

Now Stephan is totally confused. What does Nathan know Liz's connection to Dr. Ortega and himself?

Nathan coolly continues, "Oh, I remembered seeing Liz there. I have this ability to recognize familiar traits in people that they take with them into adulthood, so it was not difficult for me to recall the essence of her personality."

"Unfortunate about her need to excessively nourish her body so she might emotionally cope with all that was happening; however, I note that she has corrected that error. ..." He trails off with indifferent concern. "I shall continue."

"Actually, Liz and I spoke about our mutual encounters with Dr. Ortega and, interestingly enough, she divulged even more about her particular experiences, expanding on what she feels it all means."

Stephan is growing increasingly irritated by Nathan's arrogant knowledge of certain highly personal information about Liz and now himself. Nathan, sensing Stephan's mood, cuts to the chase.

"Dr. Ortega's death was not an accident. He was murdered by those who wished to silence him as he was about to uncover information the government wished to keep secret from the public. More importantly, Dr. Ortega was connecting the dots, I believe the saying goes, about the three of us — Elizabeth, you, and me."

"By human standards, we have unusual abilities and were individually chosen to be part of a greater endeavor. It is no mistake that we are, once again, in proximity of one another."

Stephan's anger has now turned into silent focus as he leans in to encourage Nathan to continue.

"It is my understanding that you totally know of what I speak, and that the time has now come for the three of us to begin to formulate that which we are intended to accomplish for the good of all."

Stephan, now sitting erect in his seat, nods in agreement and finds his voice again to ask Nathan... "What is it that we do now?"

"We all still have pertinent information to gather before we can implement our assignments. It is my suggestion to you that your next step is to travel to a place high in the Arizona desert, where there are many resources from which you may draw the information you seek in an effort to fulfill your destiny and complete your mission."

Stephan interrupts Nathan's monologue, "What about Liz ... and you? What are you to do? Will we be working together?"

As Nathan slowly rises from his seat, he informs Stephan that for this part of the journey he must continue on alone. It will be made clear to Stephan when the appropriate time is right and the three will be, once again, standing side by side, so to speak, in unison for the common good of man.

For now, Stephan is to talk to no one of this. Familiar advice for Stephan. Ever since he was a boy, he was constantly cautioned not to speak to anyone of his "visitors," Lupo, his sleepwalking, his special trips, his drawing, and now this!

Deep in his very being, Stephan realizes the importance of his part in all of this. There is a knowing that, despite his outward normal human life, there awaits a monumental purpose he was gifted to execute, and he intends to do just that.

As Stephan's awareness drifts back to the pub, he realizes that Nathan has left without a goodbye. A hint of a smile forms on Stephan's face as he rises to go.

Once outside, as Stephan approaches his car in the darkened parking lot, he takes a moment to glance skyward and instantly locates Sirius twinkling back at him. All is well, Stephan reassures himself. All *is* well!

Sedona

As a result of my dramatic meeting with Nathan that fateful night at the Pub, I diligently embarked on some research of my own about the high desert country in Arizona that he so emphatically suggested I explore.

I stumbled upon an area in northern Arizona that was fast becoming a hotbed of UFO activity and paranormal events. The area was called Sedona, and it was purported to be experiencing an unusually large amount of unexplained sightings and paranormal events.

Sedona was well known for attracting New Agers and freethinkers, so I felt this community would welcome my casual investigatory presence without fear of skepticism or criticism. And I was right.

I booked a flight from Washington to Colorado and then continued on to Phoenix, Arizona, which is approximately one hundred twenty miles or so south of Sedona. What little reading I did about the area hadn't prepared me fully for the magnificent beauty I encountered as I drove up "the hill," as they say, from the desert valley floor of the metro-Phoenix area in my rented car.

At an altitude of four thousand five hundred feet, this was no ordinary high-desert environment — quite the opposite. After exiting off the highway, I found myself surrounded by towering red *rock monoliths carved, no doubt, through centuries of wind, water, and natural earth shifts. It was almost impossible to fathom that this arid desert environment was once under water, with its primary inhabitants being dolphins and whales.*

Just as amazing was the red clay ground cover that was meticulously dotted with deep lush greenery of desert cacti, Ponderosa pine trees, and low brush. I remember thinking to myself, God is the Master Landscaper here, indeed.

The numerous mesas and buttes had very distinct shapes; in fact, many of these incredible formations were assigned names that perfectly fit their appearances, such as Cathedral Rock, Bell Rock, Courthouse Butte, and Coffee Pot Rock. One very popular formation totally resembled Snoopy lying on his doghouse as drawn by Charles Schultz. Amazing! But this was just the beginning of amazing.

I set aside my first few days for driving around Sedona, just to take in the magnificence of the rock formations and the clear, crisp cobalt blue skies prevalent there all year-round — and to get a feel for the area and its inhabitants.

Well, nobody warned me about the "feeling" part of being in Sedona, but I soon found out — sometimes the hard way — that I wasn't in Kansas anymore, Toto!

I purchased the usual tourist information guidebooks and noted the emphasis on hiking to the many vortexes found in the area, and their varied effects on the environment and on all living things. I was getting more and more intrigued by this magical place.

On my third day in Sedona, as I sipped my morning brew at a local coffee shop, I questioned my waiter about the purported UFO activities in the area. Without missing a beat, he pointed out a man sitting in a corner all by himself. The waiter then urged me to just casually wander on over and ask him my questions.

Before I could even mutter some inane excuse about not wanting to bother the man, the waiter had already moved back behind the counter and was busying himself with another customer.

So there I sat, trying to muster up enough gumption to get up out of my seat and meander over to this perfect stranger and pose some outlandish questions to him.

I cleared my throat as I slowly rose from my chair, and said to myself, Okay, here goes!

When I reached the man's table, I managed to mumble some meager introduction and asked if I could have a moment of his time as I had just arrived in town and was here to do some research — "Have a seat," he interrupted without even looking up at me as he sipped from a coffee mug cupped in both hands.

"Thanks," I said, and sat down.

I quickly began to formulate some kind of officious, highly intellectual dialogue in an effort to let him know I was here to research paranormal sightings in Sedona, and needed to gather some data on the mysterious events that I've heard so much about.

But before I even got my next full sentence out, he began telling me that he already knew why I was here and that he'd be happy to share whatever information I could fathom. He went on to state that I needed to keep an open mind about what he was about to reveal; otherwise, he didn't want to waste my time or his. Then he lifted his head and looked me straight in the eye, awaiting my response. I rapidly nodded my head in agreement.

As he began his monologue — I say monologue, as he made it quite clear his time was limited this particular morning, and that in order for him to give me a hint of what I came to uncover, it would be best if I kept silent and didn't ask any questions, at least for now — Wide-eyed, I nodded again in compliance and gestured with my hand for him to continue.

He said his name was Brad Phillips, and he was known around this area as the local UFO expert. He went on to tell me that over the past several years, he and a few of his close friends had unwontedly stumbled onto a bunch of unusual, unconnected sightings and encounters. What struck him most was the frequency with which these events were happening.

As a result, he had now become totally obsessed with getting to the bottom of it all. He went on to mention that he was diligent about keeping a journal of these experiences, and with a little prompting wrote several books about them, and was now sought out by other well-known international investigators seeking to pick his brain about these unusual phenomena.

Others who have had similar experiences have come to trust him and know he takes great care in recounting their paranormal events without revealing their true identities for fear of — just for fear.

One of the things I got right away was that Brad seemed to be a man of his word and that he preferred to keep a low profile, thus maintaining his integrity by not seeking publicity and, more importantly, preserving his own sanity.

He told me that what he was about to reveal would be enough for anyone to question if he was a victim of altitude sickness or just plain over the edge and totally lost his mind.

I took a chance and interrupted him just quickly enough to ask if it would be all right for me to take notes. He waived me off, saying "Not this time ... perhaps the next time we meet." Next time? This was encouraging.

Brad continued with some preliminary background of the area and how through history it has been touted as a sacred land of our Native American forefathers.

While I was paying close attention to his words, I couldn't help but be amused by the thought of his reaction when he discovers who I am, where I'm really from, and who began to visit me when I was only three.

Before I knew it, two and a half hours had passed with Brad doing all the talking. I was totally enthralled by his "tip of the iceberg" stories and hungered for more.

We agreed to meet at the coffee shop again in a couple of days. I attempted to provide him with information about where I was staying in town and how he could reach me, but he said that wouldn't be necessary — we'd find each other eventually I knew he was right.

ॐ

(Flashback)

Talk about a man on a mission, Stephan can't get enough reading materials on Sedona. Thank God the books he purchased at the local bookstores aren't very heavy reading, so he's able to pore through them in record time.

He takes advantage of what time he guesstimates he has before his next encounter with Brad to visit some of the more popular hiking areas and tourist attractions, such as The Chapel, a lovely ultramodern-designed structure built into a rock formation high upon a hill where he can see for miles and take in the panoramic view of so many other formations that simply take his breath away.

Stephan can't help but notice how peaceful he feels here, and that everyone he encounters seems to be walking around in an altered state of bliss. He takes advantage of the quietness and the plethora of opportunities to find isolated areas in which to be alone with nature and with his thoughts. Even though he has been in Sedona only a few days, he already recognizes a shift in his awareness and is very attuned to the hum of the Earth.

He feels the presence of many who have gone before him, and welcomes their kind spirits. He sits for hours deep inside one of his favorite locations called Boynton Canyon, absorbing the wisdom of the Elders who surely still inhabit this sacred space.

So deep in his own thoughts, Stephan is unaware that nightfall has begun. Even though it's midsummer, the desert temperatures drop drastically with the setting sun. Stephan reemerges back to reality and feels it best to begin his trek back to his car that's parked a few miles away.

Never planning to stay until dark, he now wishes he

had thought to bring at least a jacket and a flashlight. He did have enough presence of mind to pack plenty of water, as dehydration in the desert can happen quickly.

Reaching into his backpack for a fresh bottled water, he takes in the majestic beauty of the day's fading light that spot lights the towering formations around him.

He suddenly startles at the loud snap of a twig in the brush behind him, but then concludes the sounds are most likely made by dessert critters that are awakening for their nocturnal outings, now that the heat of the day has subsided. Smiling to himself, he feels a closeness with the earth he hasn't felt since his early days on the hillside farm in Italy. How he loved his life then.

Even though the trails are well marked by cairns which are rocks contained in chicken wire mesh, he must strain his vision to follow what he believes to be the way out of the canyon to the parking lot by the trailhead.

Then he hears it again. Only louder and closer this time.

Stephan, no longer feels safe, so he picks up his pace, all the while hoping that he's headed in the right direction toward the trailhead and the refuge of his car.

The one thing Stephan has been able to determine from the sounds behind him is that whatever is making them is on his trail — directly behind him. Tracking him?

Stephan doesn't know exactly when he became afraid, but he is now just short of a full state of panic. Propelling himself forward even faster now, he is well aware that the only other sound he hears is that of his own heavy breathing as he struggles through the brush and craggy rock.

He has totally lost the marked trail now, but the constant snapping of twigs and rustling of brush continue just over his shoulder, closing in on him swiftly.

Now in a full run, he stumbles over large rocks and red rock gravel that lie loosely underfoot. His heart pounds furiously as he hears the muffled treading of what sounds like a large animal. He knows this area is full of mountain lions, javelina, coyotes, and whatever other beasts inhabit this canyon.

Suddenly, a voice deep inside him warns to step no further. He unwittingly obeys just in time to catch himself before he is about to step off a high ridge, preventing a fall that certainly would have caused him major harm if not his death.

With his heart racing so fast that he finds it almost impossible to breathe, Stephan contemplates his next move. Does he even have one?

Before he can evaluate his options for escape, he realizes that whatever has been chasing him has stopped as well. What does that mean? Is the pursuer gone — or is it lying in wait, knowing that Stephan is trapped with no way out.

Stephan's straining eyes dart first in one direction then another. Desperate to flee yet needing a plan, he chooses the only option open to him.

Slowly he bends over to pick up a heavy rock, in preparation to fight for his life. Before he can bring his body back up to a full stand, he hears a low guttural growl coming from more than one direction and from more than one source.

Oh God! More than one! Stephan holds his breath in an effort to concentrate on the sounds that surround him. What are they? How many are there?

His question is immediately answered. Two pairs of large, yellow eyes emerge from the brush as Stephan readies himself for battle. He doesn't even have enough time to think about his fate before a third pair of eyes appear from a rock ledge just above him. Oh, my God! This is it! There's no way out!

Just then, the newest arrival looking down on Stephan

let's out a growl so deep it sends chills down his spine. But the growling is not directed at Stephan. It's aimed at the other two beasts standing before him.

Without warning, the large shadow of the animal above launches into midair and lands with a muted thud on the terrain between Stephan and the others. To Stephan's amazement, the larger animal attacks the two animals that stalked him to this perilous point.

Wishing he could block his ears from the frightening cries of battle and hideous rips of tearing flesh and flying fur, Stephan dares not drop the boulder he still holds tightly in his grasp for fear the largest of the three may decide to turn on him next.

Within minutes the other two predator's retreat, howling and yelping with obvious injury. Stephan quickly takes a deep breath as he widens his stance, gripping the boulder even tighter in his straining fingers, prepared to defend his life against the animal that remains.

As the larger animal approaches, Stephan — in a slow, deliberate motion — raises the boulder high above his head … then suddenly stops.

He becomes transfixed upon the gaze of the yellow eyes before him, and finds it difficult to bring his body to full command to heave the boulder at this threat to his very existence.

Beyond reason, Stephan is compelled to release the boulder, but not on his target. His arms aching, he drops his rudimentary weapon on the ground between himself and the approaching beast. His eyes strain to see the form about to take his life. With one last gasp for air, he exclaims: "Lupo!"

Lupo now at Stephan's feet, lowers his head, and bumps it in submission against Stephan's body while he circles. Stephan, half laughing, half crying, reaches down to pat Lupo's head and notices a warm wetness upon his fingers. He instantly concludes that Lupo is injured. Stephan joins him on the ground, hugging and caressing the wolf's body in an effort to determine the severity of his injury, and if there are others inflicted.

Lupo winces slightly as Stephan checks one of his forelegs, indicating he has, indeed, additional wounds. Despite his injuries, Lupo nips Stephan's shirt sleeve and tugs it hard, as indication for Stephan to get up. Lupo begins a retreat, imploring Stephan to follow — which he does obediently. Together, silently, the two friends walk in the darkness, only this time Stephan is confident that he will finally be led to safety.

They're Here!

The day after my hiking experience in Boynton Canyon and my reconnection with Lupo, I got a phone message from Brad Phillips that basically said: "Anything unusual happen lately? How about we meet at 9:30 a.m. at the coffee shop?" That was it! I couldn't help but wonder if this guy was a mind reader, a psychic, or just a good guesser.

At any rate, I welcomed the opportunity to meet with him again and talk in more depth about what the heck goes on in this area. While I'm not one to point fingers — after all, look at my past history — I was a bit unsure about Brad's own motives for granting me this second audience. One way or the other I was going to get that question answered before I wasted any more of my time or his.

I drove the short distance on Highway 89A from my hotel in West Sedona to meet with Brad at the now-infamous coffee café at the exact appointed hour. When I got there, Brad was already seated in his usual spot, the table in the corner. He shared with me later on that he prefers to sit at that particular table as it's sort of out of the way and he can observe all that is before him, never needing to watch his back, which he keeps to the wall. Insecure? Nope, he tells me, he just prefers it that way.

After we exchanged the mundane "How're ya doing?" and before Brad proceeded with his monologue, I decided to start the

LUPO: CONVERSATIONS WITH AN E.T.

conversation by asking him, point-blank, why he agreed to meet with me and what's in it for him. He lifted his head, which was bowed over his cup of coffee, and chuckled out loud as he commented on how he admired my directness. Then he got right to the point.

And the point for him was just this: he's been around this area for a long time and has experienced a ton of unusual happenings — not to mention the stories told to him in confidence by so many others.

As a result, he has become astute at recognizing a serious UFOer whenever he meets one, and apparently I fell into that category. If he only knew!

Satisfied with his response, I proceeded to ask my first question, with my pen poised to record his answer — which he graciously had agreed to allow this time around. He put his hand up to indicate "wait a minute" and posed a question of his own first.

"So tell me ... what happened with you yesterday?"

I was slowly becoming accustomed to his directness and not altogether shocked by his ability to "know" things in advance, so I took a deep breath and recounted my hiking experience in the canyon, with particular emphasis on Lupo.

His response was an affirmative nodding of his head and a smirk. I felt I was providing him with a confirmation of something he already knew, more than sharing my hair-raising experience.

He picked up his coffee cup, took a long, slow sip, and said, "Okay! NOW we can begin in earnest."

ॐ

(Flashback)

As Stephan takes Brad through his harrowing adventure hiking through Boynton Canyon, he can't help but notice the sincere interest of his audience. Brad never interrupts Stephan's story until almost the very end.

At the point where Stephan describes Lupo's intervention — defending him from harm by the other beasts — Brad finally breaks his silence, lifts his baseball cap higher off his forehead, fully revealing his gaze, and asks how Stephan came to call the wolf Lupo.

"I didn't," Stephan replies. "At least, I don't remember coming up with that name. I just knew that was what he wanted to be called. While growing up in Italy, it was commonplace to call the wolves in the area Lupo. I discovered later while in college that L-U-P-O also means E.T. (extraterrestrial)." Of course, Brad thinks to himself. Of course.

Stephan continues by recounting some pertinent information about himself — telling Brad where he was born, when he first encountered the E.T.'s, and what "special talents" he has of his own.

Before he realizes it, three hours have passed, and he has not yet asked one question of Brad. Instead, this meeting ends up with Brad figuring out more of who Stephan really is. Brad seems to intuitively know that in time they'll draw their own conclusions about how they can join forces to find answers about UFO and E.T. activity in Sedona, or anywhere else for that matter.

Stephan ends their talk by detailing what he believes will be his participation in bringing a more concrete understanding of the role these extraterrestrials or inter-dimensional beings have with mankind, and whether their interaction and intention is that of friend or foe.

Duly impressed and more confident than ever that he is in the presence of perhaps a genuine offshoot of an E.T., Brad asks if Stephan would like to join him for lunch at his place, which is about four and a half miles off Highway 89A.

Stephan, pumped by the invitation, is more than willing. The unlikely twosome rise from the table and exit the café to their awaiting vehicles in the parking lot, their dialogue now bursting with enthusiasm. Brad halts the information frenzy by suggesting Stephan follow him to his home, where they can continue in complete privacy.

The short drive to Brad's provides just enough time for Stephan to get hold of his excitement and formulate pertinent questions to pose to Brad before their time together comes to a close. Stephan has final exams to prepare for as graduation is just around the corner. There's yet so much to ask and so much to see. Where to begin?

Brad turns off Highway 89A onto a remote dusty road with Stephan following closely behind. With dust swirling wildly around the two vehicles, Stephan finds it difficult to keep Brad in view. Brad is driving a four- wheel-drive Jeep Cherokee, while Stephan bumps along in his compact rental car.

As the road dust settles, Stephan notices Brad has parked and is emerging from his car. He signals Stephan to park alongside his modest house. The remote area seems to suit Brad and his need for privacy, not to mention the awesome view of the red rock formations and an open vista with its prime vantage point for stargazing.

Once inside, Stephan casually walks around the sparsely furnished room decorated in vintage Southwestern style, noting the oversized telescope standing in front of a huge picture window.

As he continues to gaze about the room, his focus turns to several different models of cameras, along with a vast array of recording equipment obviously used for Brad's investigations.

"You have quite an assortment of equipment. Pretty expensive stuff, isn't it?" Stephan quips.

"Believe it or not, a lot of it is either secondhand or donated. I've only purchased a few cameras and recording devices myself. I've been really lucky to have so many generous people provide me with this kind of stuff, so I can keep digging deeper into the phenomena that interest us all."

Stephan scans the bookcase spanning the entire wall opposite the picture window and comments to Brad on the abundance of UFO and E.T. reading material that dominates the shelves.

Brad chuckles from the kitchen immediately off the great room, where he prepares lunch for them both. "If you look close, you might find one or two of my literary works in there."

Stephan counts seven books in all that bear Brad's name as author. Hanging on a paneled wall of the great room are a few plaques and framed newspaper clippings that profess Brad as one of the world's leading authorities on UFOs. "Wow! Now I really am impressed!" Stephan says.

Obviously embarrassed by all the attention, Brad announces lunch is ready, such as it is. "Come into the kitchen and pull up a chair."

Pouring them each a large class of ice-cold lemonade, he begins to provide Stephan with some additional UFO history of Sedona and the immediate surrounding towns.

Cottonwood, for example, is a small residential community approximately fifteen miles west of Sedona. Jerome is another town slightly farther west that is best known as an old mining ghost town. They both brag of some pretty strange occurrences and unusual sightings.

Stephan pulls out a mini recorder and indicates an unspoken "Can I?" to Brad as they both devour their turkey club sandwiches and pickles. Brad nods in agreement, as he knows that to take notes at this point would take too long, and besides Stephan can't eat AND write at the same time. His talents probably don't include multi-tasking at least not at that level.

Brad begins by introducing some "not-so-nice experiences that both he and others have had in an area called Sycamore Canyon, which is about thirty-three miles long, runs north and south, and is approximately one mile wide. It's a long dusty ride on a gravel road from Clarkdale — another desert community just west of Sedona.

"During the 1800s it was a major cattle-drive route, but history states that the Basque sheepherders avoided this area because of strange, giant, hair-covered creatures that were reported to roam the terrain."

"Now, here is some of the good stuff. You might want to pay particular attention to this part. There is a purported tunnel system that is located on public property between the Coconino National Forest and the Prescott National Forest. There have been reports of people hearing loud underground and aboveground drilling sounds somewhere between Clarkdale and Jerome."

"But here's the real scary stuff — hikers have been known to stumble onto military-type soldiers, some carrying what look like M-16s or some other semiautomatic pistols. The hikers have been told in no uncertain terms that they'll be shot dead on the spot if they don't turn around and leave the area."

He goes on to tell Stephan that "An Arizona State employee was hiking one day and encountered a nine-foot alien creature. There was no exchange between them, but the hiker ran nearly five miles back to his car, never to go there again. Even though he reported it to local officials and the state police, and actually demanded an investigation of this incredible sighting, he was met with strong advice to keep his mouth shut!"

Stephan shakes his head in disbelief but understands better than most the denial that others are in when it comes to paranormal experiences. Fear is a powerful emotion that tries its darndest to refute these events because they don't fit into a familiar format or context.

Stephan interrupts Brad to inquire about the reliability of his sources. Brad emphatically states that all of his stories come from extremely credible sources, such as municipal employees, retired military personnel up to and including major generals, as well as U.S. Air Force intelligence officers who have been honorably discharged.

People from all walks of life have sought Brad out to share their stories. He's talked with prominent doctors; presidents of major banks; police officers; firefighters; and clergymen who, despite their religious background, knew what they saw and had to share it with someone.

One of Brad's most memorable accounts was from the son of a military man who recounted that back in 1955, when he was about ten years of age, he saw firsthand numerous space ships and pictures of dead aliens — some looking amazingly like human children.

His father had apparently smuggled him into the base, and somehow he eluded detection as he uncovered these artifacts. His father demanded that he never speak of what he saw for fear of retribution from the military or worse.

The son obeyed this request until his father passed away several years ago. He had carried this incredible information with him in silence all these years until he felt he could share it with someone. That someone was Brad Phillips.

Stephan could totally relate to the boy's vow of silence because he, too, was often told to never speak to anyone of his strange encounters.

"Do you have a pair of hiking shoes with you?" Brad asks Stephan.

"No, but I have a pair of sneakers in the car — why?"

"Well, change into them then. I want to take you on a hike just over the ridge behind the house. Got something to show you."

It is only around two o'clock, and the Arizona desert sun is still ablaze in the afternoon sky, so they have plenty of daylight left to explore.

Brad, while quite a bit taller than Stephan, offers him one of his cotton T-shirts to wear instead of his heavy polo shirt. The temperature this time of year can reach well into the low one hundreds, so it's wise to dress lightly and be prepared to hydrate often.

Once Stephan is garbed in his hiking clothes and armed with ample bottles of water, they proceed out the front door and head up the road on foot.

After walking a short distance, Brad turns right and leads them up a steep incline that turns into a challenging vertical rock climb some two hundred feet in.

Huffing and puffing from behind, Stephan asks where the heck Brad's taking him. Brad laughs as he reaches for another foothold in the jagged rock face and tells Stephan they are almost there. "You'll soon see how it is well worth the effort."

Brad reaches the summit first and lends a hand as Stephan struggles up.

Once atop their destination, the two stand in reverence of the panoramic magnificence laid out before them. "This view is rivaled only by the Grand Canyon," Stephan says.

As far as the eye can see are majestic white and red rock formations back-dropped by a cobalt blue sky and puffy white clouds. It is most surreal to Stephan as he watches a hawk circle high above with only the sound of the wind whistling past their ears.

"Unbelievable!" Stephan sighs.

Brad responds, "Yep, as many times as I've climbed up here, I still can't get over how small and insignificant I feel in comparison to this. It's God's best work, that's for sure!"

Pulling out a pair of high-caliber binoculars, he directs Stephan to look at a point off to the southwest. "See that formation over there? The double peak? Well, one night around dusk I was up here meditating and waiting to catch the sunset when my focus was drawn to a dark object in the sky. It wasn't silver like a plane; it was black and large. It was moving at what I estimated to be a high rate of speed and was fast approaching.

"As I watched it in flight, I remember thinking, But I don't hear any engine noise. At first I thought it was because the air currents were blowing in the opposite direction, and once it passed over I'd hear the roar of the engines. But I never did."

"In fact, when it did pass directly overhead, it was quite low — maybe only two or three hundred feet above me — with no noise. Just this big looming vehicle passing overhead. I instinctively ducked, you know, like you do when you think something is lower than it actually is."

"It seemed to hover over me for a minute or two, and it had a huge wing span and no propeller blades. I've never known of a traditional aircraft to be able to hover almost completely still like that and not make any sound!"

"And then the most unbelievable thing happened. … As I lowered my binoculars to get a better look, a bright orange beam shot out of the undercarriage of the craft and encased me in a tube of light, you know?" Brad's emotions begin to rise with each word.

"Then, before I could figure out what part of the ship it was coming from or even if I should run, I guess I blacked out or something because the next thing I knew I was lying on the ground by my car in my front yard, and it was dark out. At first I thought maybe I'd fallen off the ridge, but that couldn't be right because, as you now know, the ridge is more than a mile away."

"Somehow I'd lost about six hours and ended up a mile and a half from where I stood on the ridge…"

While Brad's voice trails off Stephan gently places his hand on his shoulder. "Do you think they took you someplace?" Stephan asks.

It takes Brad a moment to realize Stephan is speaking.

"What did you just say?"

Stephan rephrases, "Do you feel you may have been abducted?"

"Yes!" Brad looks surprised by his own answer. "Up until now I've never really been able to remember what happened."

Stephan thinks this is as good a time as any to tell Brad the full truth about his own "travels," so they can both better understand the nature of the "visits" Stephan has experienced.

He begins, "As a very young boy, I was visited by what I thought were other small children, like me. Only they didn't talk, at least not out loud. We spoke to each other without saying words, and I never felt threatened or frightened when they appeared."

"I unhesitantly followed them numerous times onboard their special ships and was taken for rides high above the Earth. The funny thing was I couldn't remember what I did when I was with them, but I could draw the inside of the ships right down to the minutest detail."

"My visitations, as I would call them, continued until I was a senior in high school. It was hard enough to 'know' things that others didn't know. I would shock some and freak out others with my ability to tell them about their grandmother who was about to die or their aunt who had a tumor in her head or their dead father wanting me to pass on some message that was exactly what they needed to hear."

"But my encounters with Lupo were the most amazing. As a young child I had no fear of being in the presence of a wolf — a wild animal that for all intents and purposes could have harmed me greatly. But Lupo wasn't really what he appeared to be."

Up until now, Stephan had been extremely careful not to divulge too much information about his "specialties," but he felt safe with what he was about to share with Brad. The only other person Stephan had discussed this with in detail was Liz, and then there was Nathan, who seemed to know everything anyway.

Stephan takes in a slow breath and continues: "Remember how I told you that L-U-P-O is Italian for 'wolf,' and that I discovered it also meant E.T.? Well, in my last encounter with Lupo a few days ago, when he saved my life, what I didn't tell you was what happened just before he left me safely by my car."

Stephan tries to calculate the best way to explain and decides to just tell it the way it happened. "Once Lupo led me down to the trailhead, he stopped in his tracks. He had sustained a serious injury while protecting me from the eminent attack of the other wolves.

"As he sat on the ground, barely visible due to the darkness, all of a sudden a beam of orange light illuminated him from a source high above us both. I couldn't make out the source, but like you described when you saw that dark craft, whatever was there made no sound."

Stephan takes a sip of water to relieve his dry mouth and continues his saga, "Right before my eyes Lupo, or the image I had interpreted as Lupo, morphed into what I can only describe as the familiar shape of the childlike visitors I traveled with on those ships. The beast Lupo had turned into one of my 'friends' from my early days on the hillside farm in Italy!"

"This 'being' had an unusually large head and black slanted eyes, but no ears. He was dressed in some type of shiny metallic cloth that was silvery blue in color. Almost iridescent."

"Go on," Brad excitedly urges, who has been quietly listening up to this point.

"Without looking at me again, Lupo, or I guess I should say this being levitated up toward the source of the light, again without a sound. I stood there frozen as I watched this whole unbelievable event unfold."

"Then without warning, the light went out, the sky again darkened, and there I stood all alone in the parking lot next to my car. There was no sound, no sign of Lupo nor the light that beamed him up into the night sky."

"When I was finally able to move my legs, I opened the car door and just sat there. I don't honestly know how long I sat there, but believe me it was a while. When I felt I could drive, I fumbled my keys into the ignition and drove ever so slowly back to the main road and to my hotel room, where I collapsed onto my bed and fell instantly into a deep, deep sleep."

Brad sits there, speechless. Then he says, "I've heard many a strange tale, but this one is most unusual — and yet totally believable to me."

The two men continue to stare at each other, without speaking, then Brad lifts off his baseball cap, scratches his head, and wipes away the sweat dripping down his forehead. Then he lets out a raucous laugh. "Okay son, you got me on that one! Here's what I think. ... I think you and I need to keep talking to each other. Even after you return home. I'll tell you what else ... I think you and your 'friends' just may be the ones who can blow all this stuff right out in the open. I mean, push the edge of the envelope and get folks to understand — it's not a matter of IF they are here, it's a matter of WHY they are here!"

Stephan knows what Brad is suggesting rings true to him at his core. Now the biggest question is: HOW?

The Arizona sun is setting, and both men are weary from the day's excitement. After the two return to Brad's homestead, Stephan bids his new compadre a good evening, with the promise of more meetings and discussions to follow.

This is not over between the two men...not for a minute. The time has come for stepping up their individual investigations and pooling as much information as they can gather, so Stephan will be well armed for his next paramount task — convincing the government it's time to let the public know who walks among them, and why.

The Lobbyist

When I returned to school after my life-changing visit to Sedona, I didn't immediately know what to do with all this information.

Nathan had been incredibly astute in recommending I go there to search for additional information valuable to my mission. However, I couldn't help but wonder how he thought I could effectively merge my impending law degree with the ever-present UFO activity, in light of the government's blatant cover-up. There were hundreds upon thousands of documented accounts of alien abductions and UFO sightings, with just as many denouncements by the government stating they could all be easily explained, so what was I supposed to do with that?

While in Sedona I was in constant contact with Liz and shared with her every discovery, every event, every meeting with Brad. Liz had become more than an ally in this quest for truth. I had fallen in love with her. We both knew she would be by my side for a long time to come.

Liz had done some soul-searching of her own while I was away, and had an epiphany that changed the course of her life's direction. She told me that after graduation she was going to take some post-grad courses in psychology and that she intended to pick up where Dr. Ortega left off.

She knew her mission was to continue to guide "kids like us" and help these children find acceptance of their special abilities, so they, too, could be of value and utilize the knowledge and purpose gifted them. I thought, who better to understand these children than Liz?

As soon as I unpacked my bags, I called her to ask if we could meet as soon as possible, so we could figure out the next step in this crazy journey of ours. And, of course, I needed to talk again with Nathan to fill him in on my unbelievable trip.

To my surprise, Liz informed me no one had seen or heard from Nathan for over two weeks, and that the campus authorities had brought in local detectives to investigate his disappearance.

Deciding to put Nathan's MIA (missing in action) aside for the time being, Liz and I reviewed what we knew so far, and thought it best to sleep on it to let the dust settle (Arizona desert notwithstanding).

I did know this: I was on a fast track I couldn't get off of even if I'd wanted to.

My encounters with my "friends" and Lupo were big enough events unto themselves, but this new twist of my experience in Sedona along with my meetings with Brad Phillips left little doubt I needed to continue my research — thus arming myself with as much ammunition available for what I needed to do next.

So for the next several weeks, I isolated myself after classes, going to either the library or the confines of my dorm to read everything ever written about encounters with UFOs, abductions, and the government's continued denial of these types of phenomena.

Even though Brad expounded on the government's unmovable posture concerning UFOs, I was hoping against hope that his bias was unfounded and that, in the greater scheme of things, the government was finally at a point of acknowledgement of their existence — actually encouraging people to step forward with their stories. How naive I was.

LUPO: CONVERSATIONS WITH AN E.T.

(Flashback)

His eyes beyond weary from endlessly reading accounts of UFO sightings, alien encounters and abductions, Stephan succumbs to fatigue and reluctantly loosens his grip on the report in his hand and lets it drop to the carpet of his dormitory floor.

He drifts into a fitful slumber, as his mind refuses to stop its incessant analyzing and postulation. When Stephan awakes but a few hours later, he bolts upright in half consciousness and proclaims out loud, "Oh, my God ... that's it! Of course!"

Ignoring the lateness of the hour, or more correctly the earliness of the day, he dials Liz's phone number as he struggles to clear away any cobwebs that remain in his head.

While Liz is just as committed as he in their purposeful journey, he reminds himself just how much she enjoys her beauty sleep and that disturbing her in the wee hours of the morning holds the strong probability of her not being in the same frame of excitement; however, he continues to dial.

"Hello? ..." Liz's raspy voice responds to the telephone's urgent summoning.

"Liz! Liz! I've got it! I can't explain right now how I got it ...but I've got it!" His voice explodes with enthusiasm.

"Wha — Who ... Stephan, is that you? This better be good, Preppy, or —" She interrupts herself with a yawn as she attempts to become more awake.

"I'm on my way over. Put on some coffee, some very strong coffee. We're going to need it. I'll be there in ten minutes!" He slams the phone down and before Liz can reply," "Sure, Okay", Stephan is gone.

Liz rubs here eyes in the hopes the numbers on her digital clock can't be right as she struggles to raise her uncooperative body from its restful pose. "Coffee, coffee, coffee ..." she mumbles, shuffling her way to the small kitchen located next to her bedroom. She flips on the kitchen switch and cries, "Good Lord!" at the intensity of the light that floods over her.

Coffee started, she stares blankly out the window over the sink, watching for Stephan's car. Believing she has a few moments before his arrival, she hurries to the bathroom to wash her face and brush her teeth. She doesn't care how much she loves this man, she can't greet him with morning breath and half-asleep eyes. She laughs to herself.

The loud banging on her front door announces his arrival, and she hurries to open it, not so much in anticipation of Stephan but to quiet him before he wakes up the whole building.

He hurries past her, blowing an indifferent air kiss her way as he reaches for a coffee mug hanging under the cupboard. Cocking her head to one side as she walks toward him, she asks: "Okay, what the heck is this all about?" He risks her growing impatience by taking one more big gulp of coffee, then he begins.

"Last night I could barely keep my eyes open while I was reading through some dull, redundant materials the government had written pretty much denouncing anything and everything that's been reported on UFO sightings to a small investigative task force they created called Blue Book."

"It goes on to explain that after all the hoopla coming out of the purported episodes in the now-infamous Area 51 in Nevada and the accounts of captured aliens in Roswell, New Mexico, they have concluded beyond a reasonable doubt that there's a manmade explanation for everything. Big surprise, right?"

"They go on to denounce all of it and how the public's manic need to engage their fantasies by bringing Buck Rogers and the Star Trek adventures into reality has caused a gosh darn UFO epidemic! As I drifted off to sleep, I laughed to myself and thought, Man! You have no idea!" Stephan laughs."

Liz knows that to ask Stephan any questions at this juncture will be futile, so she nods and gestures for him to continue.

"So I fall asleep and begin to have these really vivid dreams. Nothing like when I'm about to have a visitation — quite the opposite. "

"I recognize on some level that I am, in fact, dreaming, but I am also observing the dream from outside myself. Does that make any sense?"

"Go ... go on, Stef," she urges.

"All of a sudden I'm standing in this huge room filled with people. I mean a huge room, like a rotunda or some other auditorium with a circular dais and sectioned seating. There are flags representing every country known to man flying all around the circumference of the room."

"I watch a man as he approaches the podium and slams down a gavel, which brings a hush to the crowd. Then I begin to hear his words. He is introducing a very important speaker seated just behind him, who then rises and takes his place before this assembly."

"In my dream I'm straining to make out the figure as he moves closer to the podium, and then I see — the speaker is me! I am speaking before the World Council of the Humanities!" Stephan concludes with excitement."

Liz stares for a moment then responds, "Of course! Exactly!" They both chime in together as they think aloud: "Is there anyone who has done this before on such a controversial subject as UFOs?"

They begin a frantic chatter, sometimes speaking over each other, about needing to figure out how to obtain an audience before the World Council of the Humanities, when the "Eureka" moment occurs to them simultaneously... Stephan needs to become a lobbyist, with his agenda being complete disclosure by the government of the existence of

UFO activity — thus bringing a halt to the cover-up! But this is just a fraction of their mission; the more urgent part is to bring awareness as to WHY the aliens are here.

They both stop mid-sentence and look into each other's eyes and calmly declare," "This is it! This is what we are to do!"

With that, Stephan pours himself another cup of coffee while Liz hurriedly boots up her computer, all the while fumbling through her desk drawers for pen and paper so they can begin the ardent process of submitting his application to become a lobbyist.

As the hours go by, instead of appearing fatigued, Stephan seems exhilarated, not to mention wired from all that caffeine he has consumed.

Ultimately, Liz announces she has to get dressed for class, and Stephan reluctantly acknowledges that he has a pre-exam study group to meet up with. He informs her that he'll go to the campus library later to continue his fact-finding on how to proceed in becoming a lobbyist. He knows it won't happen over night, so there's no time to lose.

It never crosses Liz's mind that Stephan might not be truly ready for this. She just knows it's the next logical step in what they came here to do.

Before departing, Stephan gently brings Liz to his chest in a close embrace. He looks deep into her piercing blue eyes and tells her how much he loves her and how they are about to embark on one of the most exciting parts of their journey together. Liz smiles from ear to ear and says, "I go where you go. Bring it on, Preppy!"

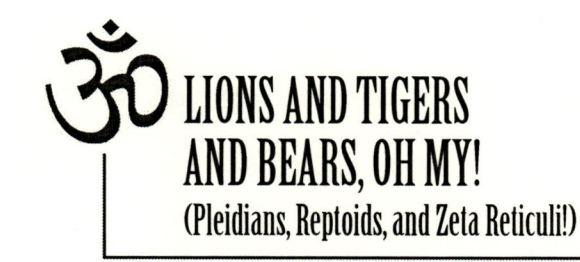

ॐ LIONS AND TIGERS AND BEARS, OH MY!
(Pleidians, Reptoids, and Zeta Reticuli!)

*T*he baby-boomer era produced not only changes in consciousness but gave rise to intense focus and concentrated awareness to the possibilities of other life forms. Non-human — not us — life forms.

Nothing made that so clear as the master creation of television. A decidedly technological phenomenon for its day that brought families together to gaze endlessly hour after hour at a small box that produced black-and-white images for our amusement and occasionally our intellect.

While most people viewed this wonderful invention as a major advancement in modern technology, I on the other hand, found it an amusing, almost primal building blocks — like Legos, if you will. Don't get me wrong; for lack of something better to do, I, too, was glued to the "boob tube" as visions of game shows, comedy hours, and live dramas flashed before my very eyes.

But what drew my sincere interest were the initial feeble portrayals of space travel and the introduction of "aliens" right into our living rooms. As corny as it was presented, the accuracy of its delivery was somewhat comical, at least to me.

While programs like Flash Gordon and, in later years, Lost in Space lacked credibility — with their humorous attempts to lure their audience with the portent of life on other planets, space *travel, and alien beings — they ended up being a driving force that ultimately, if not deliberately, bred fear and hostility toward whatever else lay outside our galactic box.*

The mere thought of other beings that looked horrific and threatened our peaceful existence couldn't be any further from the truth, in my opinion. That's not to say there aren't negative beings, whether here in our dimension or in nonphysical, whose intent for a peaceful coexistence differs from ours. However, that old expression "one bad apple ..." certainly applies here.

Around the time Star Trek *was introduced to TV Land, at least those writers proved to display some level of intelligence and took responsibility to incorporate plausible scenarios of a less threatening nature. They also introduced the idea of a Galactic Federation of sorts that governed the unruly aliens and stood fast in mediation and arbitration for the purpose of joining together beings of difference in an effort to promote peace and harmony amongst the shared space of our galaxies.*

But the real heroes, the ones who thought up this whole idea of life on other planets besides our own and introduced the plausibility of technologies beyond our limited thinking, were sheer geniuses.

By the time Star Wars, Close Encounters of the Third Kind, *and* E.T. *were made, the mass consciousness was ready, willing, and able to acknowledge the seriousness of the subject matter, and began recognizing that the governments around the planet were in some sort of conspiring agreement to continue to let the public believe that interaction with these beings was detrimental to their very existence.*

Star Wars *kept the "good guy/bad guy" conflict alive and well, leaving fantasy as its genre and fear in its wake.*

Close Encounters of the Third Kind *was the breakthrough movie that not only took on the monumental task of acknowledging the government's cover-up policies but introduced recreations of actual nonviolent encounters through special effects and drama that had audiences everywhere unable to deny this fictional story was possible and most assuredly plausible.*

E.T., however, was the closet depiction to the reality of what some galactic neighbors are about and that they mean us no harm. It is the E.T. beings that I, personally, interacted with in my younger years while living on the farm in Italy.

I had a special fondness for the movie E.T. and a profound appreciation of Steven Spielberg for having the courage to take such a giant step in the movie-making industry by venturing out of the proverbial box and portraying our alien neighbors as the gentle, benevolent beings that some of them are.

More amazingly, the physicality of the E.T. character was so brilliantly — dare I say, accurately — depicted that it caused me to ponder if Mr. Spielberg had, himself, been the participant in a close encounter of any kind.

Unfortunately, Mr. Spielberg took a one-hundred-eighty-degree turn from those types of films when he recently directed the updated version of War of the Worlds, *undoing all the positive imaging he had brought to the masses over two decades before.*

Just as we have many cultures and races here on Earth, so it is in this expansive galaxy of ours. We are not made up of only whites, blacks, Indians, and Asians — just to name a few. There are innumerable cross-cultures and hybrids walking around in human form.

The majority of alien beings come from Pleiades, Orion, Lyra, Vega, Sirius, Arcturus, Andromeda, and Cassiopeia (home of the praying mantis race of tall Greys).

The star beings that receive the most notoriety are the Greys (Zeta Reticuli Type A — who are more aggressive — and Type B — who are less hostile and display miraculous feats with their higher technologies).

Next come the Pleidians, also known as the Nordics/Swedes, who are here to observe and not interfere, at least not yet. It is purported that Pleidians appear most like humans and, because of this, can walk among us without detection. They are prophesized to be the ones who will ultimately bring humans into the light. They communicate telepathically; travel from place to place through a tube system; and are primarily vegetarians, although they do occasionally eat meat. They are in control of their own health, so no medicines or technological interventions are utilized. Their skin is whiter and smoother than human skin, and they have a seven-hundred-year life span.

Finally, there are the Reptoids, which are bird-like reptilian entities. They are anywhere from six- to eight-foot bipedal reptilians with large, yellow, vertical pupils. These entities have been part of the Earth since its beginnings and were best described in history as being prevalent in the now-famous dinosaur era. But, like I said, that's only three of uncountable others.

The most "popular" abduction tales are those of the Greys. I have firsthand knowledge of the Greys (Type B), and, unfortunately, some of the more negative beings of their species (Type A) have been instrumental in keeping the fear factor in the hearts of mankind.

The irony of the Zeta Reticuli is that their planet is located in the same Orion constellation as Sirius, my star home. Some theorize that the Greys are the observers and perhaps the creators of this third dimensional holographic program called the human experience on planet Earth.

It is speculated that this is only one of many in the grid of realities and that we humans are encoded and are guided by them through our evolution. Because the Zeta Reticuli are a dying species due to over-cloning that has weakened them, it is their intention to crossbreed with humans in an effort to create a better species. So ask yourself: Why, then, would they destroy the program?

My encounters have always been ones of cooperation. While I initially interacted with the smaller Greys, I continued my "education," as it were, with the taller Greys, whose height ranges anywhere from seven to nine feet. They also have the distinction of a large nose, which the smaller Greys do not possess.

I was never forced to go anywhere I didn't want to go. Once I adjusted to the process of interaction and how I came and went from one reality to another, I eagerly participated in their schooling and welcomed our encounters.

Very early on, it was made crystal clear to me that my participation in this part of the evolutionary journey was but a next step in what would be for the greater good of all — mankind and non-mankind.

LUPO Speaks

When I look back on this incredible journey and all that has happened thus far, the most amazing thing to me is that it's really just begun.

Becoming a respected, credible lobbyist was no small feat. It took years of internship and research coupled with a ton of rejection and heartache causing me to wonder if this endeavor was ever going to be brought out into the light, let alone successful.

Blazing a new trail in this untried arena of UFO and E.T. awareness, I was fortunate, indeed, to have amassed people of like mind who saw the value of taking the huge risk and stepping out of the proverbial box for the sake of humanity and its future.

The people and the star beings I've encountered along this journey are but a few in an unknown number who hold a common vantage point, a positive perspective of a beautiful, harmonious coexistence in this brief episode we call life.

As much as I think I've learned, the knowledge and the immense insight I have gleaned through those interactions are but a minute particle of ALL THAT IS!

What I held as my perception proved to be an ever-changing metamorphosis of realities. As I crossed back and forth from dimension to dimension, confused for a while as to which one was real, I came away with my own truth that they are ALL real! It just *depends on where you hold your focus at that moment, I guess.*

I don't know how or why I, like so many others, were chosen to assist this planet and its inhabitants to expand their thinking by becoming leading-edge creators of a new way of being, but I am beyond grateful for my participation in this evolutionary process in the hope of manifesting a world, a galaxy, an infinitum of expansive joy and peace.

ॐ

(Flashback)

As Stephan prepares for his trip to New York to speak before the World Council of the Humanities, he has a moment of panic. How can I possibly articulate all that needs to be said in such a way that it is truly heard, he torments to himself.

He decides to clear his head by taking a walk along the riverbank that borders his home. It is always so peaceful and uninterrupted there, and that's exactly what he needs right now.

He reaches for his trusty handheld recorder, pops in a new mini cassette, and pockets two more so he can immediately record his thoughts and strategies for the most important lobby of his life — no, mankind's existence.

With summer over, the early morning chill announcing fall's impending arrival prompts Stephan to take along a lightweight jacket. Walking along aimlessly in search of the right spot to settle and focus, his thoughts turn to Liz — how blessed he feels to have her love and how vital her role has been through all of this incredible journey.

He flashes back to his earliest memories of her sitting in Dr. Ortega's office, munching on a large bag of potato chips. He marvels at the first adult impression she made on him when she boldly bounded into his class on The Study of

Psychological Phenomenon that first year in college.

He recalls first being drawn to her outlandish sense of humor, her defiant — dare he say, "cocky arrogance" — with the professor as she constantly challenged and baited him into one of her nobody-can-win debates on the probability of life on other planets. If only Professor Nordstar were still alive today and could talk with her now!

Stephan's reverie is broken by a morning jogger passing by with his leashed dog panting in tow. Stephan stops walking to look around and spies a welcoming cluster of maple trees whose leaves are just beginning to turn their seasonal hue.

He chooses to sit beneath the largest in the group of trees that face the river's great expanse. The sun has now risen sufficiently in the morning sky, so its warming rays are beginning to be felt. Stephan sighs deeply, not knowing where to begin.

He momentarily changes his focus to observe a bright yellow kayak maneuvering gently down this placid section of the river. He sighs once again as he gently closes his eyes for but a moment. Then … he feels it!

At first the vibration is barely noticeable. His conscious mind rapidly concludes it's an airplane passing overhead at a low altitude. No need to open his eyes and interrupt his blissful moment.

"Hm-m-m-m, Hm-m-m-m-m, H-m-m-m-m."

Now the sound becomes ever louder: "H-m-m-m-, H-M-M-M, H-M-M-M-M, H-M-M-M-M!" Stephan can actually feel the ground vibrating in harmony beneath him as he sits beneath the tree.

Suddenly, Stephan is engulfed in "OH-M-M-M-M-M-M, OHM-M-M-M-M, OH-M-M-M-M, OHM-M-M-M!" and finds it impossible to ignore.

This sound has become innately familiar to Stephan, so he remains seated, eyes still shut as he relaxes even more into the deafening sound. "OOOH-MMMMM, OOOH-MMMMM,

OOOH-MMMM, OOOH-M-M-M-M-M!"

Louder and louder the vibration tones take Stephan deeper and deeper into himself. With a whoosh, he senses himself speeding through a weightless tunnel. Not falling or plummeting, just moving forward at warp speed.

All of a sudden the forward momentum ceases, and Stephan's body begins to float downward, where it finally lands softly on a solid surface.

Stephan slowly opens his eyes and looks around to orient himself to his new surroundings. To his amazement, what he sees is a similar scene to the one where he just sat but a few moments ago, only this environment's appearance is definitely altered from the other.

The colors are florescent in spectrum. Stephan observes the same yellow kayak passing before him as it had done before, only this time the water pushed out by the oars of the boatman glows iridescent blue, green, and yellow.

As Stephan attempts to adjust his vision to take in this new look, he glances around toward the cluster of trees that surround him and observes some leaves as they silently fall. They, too, are encompassed by an iridescent aura, this time of red, orange, and green. They seem to emit a muted musical chime as they lightly touch the ground: "Bing ... bing ... bing."

This has to be one of the most beautiful places he's ever seen. But wait a minute ... there is another sound emanating from the low-lying shrubs to his right.

He moves his gaze slowly to the direction of the sound. His squinted eyes attempt to focus in on the moving object as it emerges from the greenery in slow motion.

It doesn't take long for Stephan to recognize this familiar figure and shout, "LUPO!"

Stephan stands to greet his old friend, whom he hasn't seen in a long while — not since his rescue in Boynton Canyon. Stephan abruptly stops in mid-stance. As Lupo's canine form

LUPO: CONVERSATIONS WITH AN E.T.

approaches, it immediately begins to morph right before Stephan's eyes into ... Nathan?

While Stephan's brain struggles to accept what his eyes are interpreting, Lupo's morphing continues. What briefly stood walking toward him first as Lupo, then as Nathan, now stands directly before Stephan as ... the "Visitor" — with oversized head and black sunglass-like eyes.

The ever-so-tall, lean figure, with no ears and pencil-thin lips, bows his head in greeting to Stephan, who is frantically blinking in disbelief.

Before Stephan can truly grasp any of this, a gentle voice commands him to sit down. Feeling weak in the knees, he has no problem complying.

Stephan's next thoughts are: Am I dead? ... Am I even breathing? ... I don't think I'm breathing!

"Of course you're still breathing, and NO you are NOT dead!" replies the being standing erect before him. "There is no death, anyway, but that discussion will come at another time," the voice replies to his thoughts.

Stephan's gaze is now fully upon this being who apparently is the source of the voice. He begins to ease into it all and silently declares to himself that he's having one of his "visits." Isn't that right? he thinks.

"Yes, you are correct. Welcome, Stephan. It has been some time since our last encounter. We have much to discuss, so listen carefully. The time has come for revelation."

As Stephan holds his seated position, the alien being remains standing before him. Floating before him, actually, as Stephan notices the being's lower extremities never quite touch the ground.

Stephan speaks: "You are familiar to me, yes? We've met many times before, haven't we? What name do I call you?"

The voice answers: "'Lupo' is fine. Our dialogue this time will be entirely on the task at hand. It is crucial that your thoughts remain focused, so you may relay this information accurately to the others. Do you understand?"

Stephan's reply is a strong and steady "Yes!"

Lupo: *When you came to this Earth School as a very young child, you were carefully and deliberately positioned in a place of easy access for us to watch and meet with you unnoticed. Your Earth family were simple, unsophisticated humans who were unknowing of beings such as we and others like us. They were riddled with foolish superstitions and myths about that which they could not explain, yet perfect for our purpose.*

Stephan: *Why was it, then, that I had to leave and go to that awful orphanage and suffer such abuse with that foster family before coming to live with my adopted family in America?*

Lupo: *We didn't have much control over that, Stephan. The time you ran into the night to find me, to find the entity you refer to as Lupo, so frightened your caregivers that they feared for your safety, living with them on the hillside.*
While they wanted you to remain with them, their concern for what was best for you left them no alternative but to contact the orphanage in the hope of providing you with a permanent family as a safe haven.
We were not allowed to intercede for fear of being discovered or, worse, eliminated from the project. Your stay at the orphanage and with the other unkind Earth family was unfortunate, but we needed a little more time to secure better arrangements.

Stephan: *You mean you were responsible for getting my adopted family and me together?*

Lupo: *Exactly. We even added in a bit of your Earth humor by finding a family whose original name was Lupiano but Americanized it to Wolf. Did it not catch your notice? My species* is not generally known for exhibiting emotions of any kind, let alone humor; however, we found it intriguing to leave you clues such as this one, so as to follow your observations and discoveries.

 Stephan: Actually, that one didn't escape my notice. But I've got a question for you. If you were in control of bringing me back and forth for our visits, how was it then that when it was time to return me, you weren't a bit more exact in your coordinates?
 I got into a lot of trouble for my "sleepwalking" and was constantly tied up or locked up, only to be found in the early morning hours outside of buildings or on the lawn of wherever I was staying. I was beaten many times for my disappearing act.

 Lupo: Admittedly your Earth density still holds some mystery for us. We continue to experiment with our calibrations, vectors, and coordinates for proper replacements; we are not yet perfect, as you say.
 But let us discuss your outrage at our minor errors another time and resume our discussion of more urgent matters.

 Stephan: Minor errors? Those minor errors nearly got me locked up in a loony bin! If it hadn't been for Dr. Ortega, I might have been placed in a hospital somewhere with the key thrown away! Speaking of Dr. Ortega, was he part of all this?

 Lupo: Not exactly. He was allowed to have access to you and the others. ...

 Stephan: Like Liz?

 Lupo: Like Elizabeth, but Dr. Ortega needed to go so much deeper with his studies of your kind that it became necessary to introduce Nathan so as to heighten the intensity of the investigation of children such as you.
 Unfortunately, there are those in your government who felt

uneasy with Dr. Ortega's unanticipated diligent detective work, so once he got too close to uncovering some of their secrets, he needed to be eliminated.

You see, it was never their intention to let Dr. Ortega do anything more with you children than pacify your families, teachers, and anyone else who questioned your claims of abductions or your extraordinarily high level of psychic ability.

So we allowed Dr. Ortega a way to uncover just enough evidence to substantiate the necessity for the therapy sessions, thus providing a vehicle to cloak the increasing interest the government was demonstrating regarding you children.

It provided a failsafe for all of you to be pushed under the carpet, so to speak, so as not to encourage further examination of the growing phenomenon by the public at large.

So many children were being brought to Earth with their special abilities, and their detection was becoming obvious. Someone deemed it necessary to label them according to their unique abilities. They have been called Crystal Children or Indigo Children. Semantics ... just semantics.

Dr. Ortega was closely monitored, not only by government officials but by us as well. The information he gathered was only "smoke and mirrors" designed for the ultimate purpose of providing a distraction for the government. More accurately, the destruction of information.

We had no need to study you and the others, simply to instruct and guide you toward your ultimate humanitarian and galactic purpose.

    Stephan: *Why didn't you stop them?*

    Lupo: It wasn't time yet. We thought it best to protect you children by allowing the events to unfold in the manner in which they did, so that you and they might be perceived as "less special" and resume a semi-normal childhood, with the exception of our visits. It was always our intention to reduce the number of *visits for a bit until you got older so as to allow the human part of your experience to flourish and complement a balance between your duality.*

Stephan: *There would never be anything even close to normal for us. I remember the visits became more serious and not at all so playful.*

Lupo: *Indeed. Just as human growth experiences expand on Earth, we too have a propensity for more serious matters to be dominant.*

Stephan: *So, WE children/adults have been groomed right from the start? You've orchestrated pretty much most of our lives right up to this moment?*

Lupo: Accurately stated. We knew even before you emerged into physical form who you were to become and what role each one of you would play in the execution of this mission born of the Galactic Federation.
You were chosen, all of you, for your special abilities, individual personalities, and unique talents to be positioned throughout the galaxy to live, learn, and grow amongst the species until this moment of revelation.
I must add that all of you always had the free will to not participate. We gave you that option after each and every time of visit. It was not our intention to utilize your abilities against your will.
Upon the conclusion of each visit, each encounter, you were always asked if you wished to cease your involvement, to have your memories of any of this erased forever, and to resume a life of your choosing. For it is your birthright. You and the others made it clear that you wished to continue. And so it is!

Stephan: *Just how many of us are there? Enough to*

make a difference?

Lupo: *The numbers are vast. There are many who have walked amongst the Earthlings for centuries.*

In the greater galaxy, where the measurement of time is not linear such as it is on Earth, it is almost impossible to describe in a format that you can understand. For clarity, let it be enough to use the Earth analogy of the theory of Critical Mass or the Hundredth Monkey. Does that help you?

Stephan: *Yes, that's clear. Now it comes down to the most important question of all: How do I convey the importance of what is about to happen when I go before the World Council of the Humanities?*

Lupo: *I will speak, you will listen. When I am through speaking, it will then be appropriate for you to request any further clarification. Let us begin.*

We and others like us have been part of Earth's beginnings. First as observers, still as observers. The interaction, while seemingly new to Earthlings, has gone on before. For as I mentioned, there is no linear time throughout space. Only here.

There were those from other galaxies of a more aggressive nature who attempted to dominate; however, the Federation intervened with swift and cataclysmic results. For example, I believe you refer to one such era as the Ice Age.

Earth is a living entity unto itself. It is source energy at its best. It breathes, thrives, and purges. Natural disasters are nothing more than Mother Earth eliminating that which no longer serves her well-being. The humans caught in that elimination are not unfortunate in their placement but destined, if you will, to fulfill their mission in non-third dimension. They ascend when they do, as they do, when all is in order.

There are many species that walk the earth, as do you. On Earth it is you, the human, who dominates and exhibits the higher intellect. For all others, their role is strictly lower vibration.

In the greater expanse known to you as the Universe, it is quite different. For example, the entities you refer to as insects and reptiles, while small and insignificant and most annoying on planet Earth, are a superior intelligent species with higher technologies that man has never seen the likes of. They chose to be part of this experiment as a subspecies rather than a dominant one.

That is not to say there aren't those in the infinite who would like to dominate; they are simply rebuffed from completing their intent by the powerful rule of the Federation. It is by their grant that other star beings are able to partake in this experiment.

For most, domination is not the intent, although your governments would like to portray quite the opposite for their own suspect reasons.

While there are many who govern human societies with the aid of beings less focused on Earth's continuation, there are just as many in power who are willing to listen and have already set the wheels in motion for the upheaval of dysfunctional dominance.

Right now, there are groups merging into a powerful network for positive change. Humans resist change as it is an unknown with no discernible texture. Its success is not assured, so those in power keep the populous in fear as it is an effective means of holding them in denial and thus cloaking the truth.

Humanity needs to regulate its activity to better harmonize with the ecosystem. The people of Earth are ready for the elimination of harmful environmental toxins that help line the pockets of the greedy. They are ready for one government chosen by the masses, with currency no longer being regulated by those in power, but empowering those in need to generate their own form of exchange.

In Pleiades, for example, there is no need for currency. They share resources with all, based on contribution to society as a whole. So the responsibility rests solely on the being to either prosper or be accountable for their lack. Simple.

The human formation of religions, social structures, governments, and the like, are but negotiated agreements by those who hunger to dominate the masses. While it is not unreasonable to prefer order over chaos, it is the manner in which the order is established that dictates the outcome for the general good of all.

The Galactic Federation has allowed intervention when and only when there is threat of annihilation of the planet or a populous at large. In more recent times, intervention has been allowed in an effort to keep nuclear weapons with capabilities of mass destruction in their silos, never to be launched nor reach their intended targets.

Earth was created as an experimental oasis, a stopping-off point for the continuum of leading-edge thinkers. Nowhere else in the galaxy is there a place such as Earth that provides harmonious beauty and a soothing environment for beings who experience sensually; that is, with senses of auditory, vision, smell, taste, and touch.

Perhaps one of the most significant Earth experiences that is devoid in most other planetary environments is that of emotion. It is considered a point of weakness by other star societies, yet warrants closer investigation and evaluation for its usefulness.

And so it was that the Galactic Federation deployed emissaries from numerous dimensions, by invitation only, to take part in this experiment.

In response, planets such as your star family on Sirius evaluated young candidates, some in vitro; encoded the transmitter, your human brain; positioned these new lives around the planet at different stages of its evolution; then observed the results. A sort of holographic experimentation program.

Essential knowledge has not been erased from each candidate, but has been implanted deep, so you may use this Earth School to find ways to discover it. You and others like you were key elements in assisting the transformation of life to new levels of the Earth's healing.

This transformation process is one of healing your separateness. The Federation formed a partnership with other star beings to assist the enlightening of humanity, so it may move more completely into a course of wise action.

It goes without saying that there are numerous uninvited entities that feign observation while their intention is interference and, to use a human vernacular, upset the apple cart.

You and others like you chose this Earth School journey because you accepted the challenges of participation in this lifetime in the hopes of redirecting the current evolutionary shifts on your planet. With guiding influence of the Federation, your accepted larger role is to stabilize Earth's living environment.

This is a time of rejuvenation. You are to use your abilities and talents to heal the Earth. There is no one single truth.

I will say this, the program is not in jeopardy of termination. Far from it. We all have much to learn from this and so it is then ... the program will continue.

There is much that has been assimilated, reviewed, and concluded.

While the experiment began with individual assignments, the conclusion is that separateness is useless and of no benefit. Joining together as one has proven to be of infinite value for the common good of all. And so it is that our message to those on Earth is to no longer separate from one another as your true power lays within the larger YOU.

This evolutionary period of renewal and stabilization is designed to expand awareness of sources less familiar, with the ultimate result being one of harmony of purpose.

So, I am complete. Go now, Stephan. The world awaits your contribution."

ॐ Imagine

Preparing for my speech before the World Council of the Humanities was the ultimate culmination of my journey, this far. But only the beginning of what was to be.

Knowing how unique I was and finding others "like me" gave credence to my existence. What I wasn't sure of was how I would become one of many voices that could ultimately change the world as we know it. How could I live up to such a responsibility? It was overwhelming, yet I knew I would give it my best shot.

The human side of me had doubts, fears, and a million questions. That "other" part of me was confident and all knowing. This duality made being Me a real challenge.

As I looked back on my journey from my first recollections of living with my foster family on the hillside farm in Italy, I couldn't help but wish I could regain the innocence and simplicity life offered back then. Being ... just being! Living each moment – in the moment.

Coming to terms with my abilities and my connection with others like me was a monumental task, to say the least. But convincing my family and friends that what was happening to me was nothing to be feared was nearly impossible.

The jury is still out with most of my immediate family on all of this, but I will say, the one person who shocked me by staying *somewhat open to the possibilities was my dad. I thought he'd be the last one to accept any of it, but he genuinely keeps a crack in the door open because of his powerful love for his son. My mom just keeps walking around the house blessing herself and muttering some prayerful verbiage that will keep me and those around me safe from harm. So be it!*

Most of my childhood chums have moved on, and we don't talk much anymore. To tell you the truth, I think they feel it best to give me a wide berth these days. My stories and talents were cool when we were kids, but unexplainable and just plain weird as adults. My only wish is that they will remember the wonderment of the experiences I shared with them while growing up together, and be receptive to their own children's "special talents" because it is this new generation that holds the key to positive global change.

I'm still in touch with some of my college buddies, but mostly the ones who were involved in my lobbying efforts. A seasoned lobbyist is capable of grabbing the attention of not only financial backers but a significant entourage of powerful supporters along the way. I was blessed with obtaining both.

With the subject matter of UFOs, extraterrestrials, and the granddaddy of all — the Great Government Cover-up, I was blazing a new trail in this industry and for the history books. Luckily, I had gained the confidence and respect of a small handful of "believers" who volunteered their time and talents to the cause. I am forever grateful for their generosity, compassion, and insight of what can be.

It goes without saying that Brad Phillips was an integral part of this process, so I invited him to join me and be prepared to answer some pretty tough questions. I was amused to see when I picked him up at the airport that he was laden with boxes upon boxes of written testimonials and recordings ... just in case. I could always count on Brad to rise to the occasion.

With such a monumental task put before me, Liz and I couldn't have possibly accumulated the research materials all by ourselves. No way!

These volunteers were instrumental in compiling the hundreds upon thousands of written testimonials from key witnesses ranging from retired military personnel, government officials, prominent physicians, bankers, corporate bigwigs, celebrities, commercial pilots, all the way through to the working-class men and women who had firsthand accounts of UFO and extraterrestrial events since 1947, which earmarked the official beginning of the investigation.

As long as the government keeps the public busy focusing on the debate of the existence of UFOs and extraterrestrials, then the real issues of why they are here and what the government's sinister role is in their cover-up remain enigmas. More importantly, politicians can continue with their global environmental challenge for power, coercion, greed, and corruption in earnest. ("Watch the right hand, so you don't see what the left hand is doing" is their mantra.)

I had the undaunted task of ripping off the government's mask of illusion, and presenting a new way of perceiving our galactic neighbors as not only the high technological gurus they are but as benevolent emissaries capable of elevating our evolution into the fifth world. A challenging concept at best.

Just imagine a world united in purpose — a co-mingling of idealisms for the common good of man. Recalling the powerful lyrics from John Lennon's song "Imagine": "You may say I'm a dreamer, but I'm not the only one. I hope someday you'll join us.... And the world will live as one."

When the moment of truth arrives and the impact of my speech before the World Council of the Humanities is felt around the world, then and only then will I pass the gauntlet.

ॐ

(Flashback)

His speech before the World Council of the Humanities was more than Stephan could have ever envisioned. Not only did he have the full attention of the entire assembly for over four hours but what was born of this amazing moment in time held the portent of a new life, a birthing of a new era for not only the people on Earth but throughout the galaxy.

As Liz and Stephan settle into their hotel room, Liz is clearly exhausted and draws herself a soothing bubble bath before retiring to bed. Stephan is beyond exhilarated and sits in a chair by the window overlooking this amazing city of millions, in awe of the day's unfolding. Pinch me!

As the flow from the bathtub faucet fills a well-deserved respite for Liz, Stephan relives the highlights of the day. He smiles to himself remembering being poised and ready for his announcement by the Majority Leader of the Dias and how this depicted exactly what he had seen in his prophetic dream the night he decided to become a lobbyist. It all seems so long ago … so long ago.

Standing before the mass assembly of the Council, not to mention the hordes of international media, Stephan recalls feeling but a fleeting moment of panic — would he say enough? Would he be able to share his experiences in a manner that would be taken seriously by the Council? Could he open the minds of this small representation of humanity to embrace the opportunity to be the ones to change the course of history for mankind and beyond?

Reliving that moment makes Stephan shiver. Then he recalls the calm that washed over him as he cleared his throat and began thanking the assembly for this opportunity.

Somehow the words flowed as he spoke evenly, confidently, and articulately. He felt altered in his state of consciousness — a puppet, if you will, to words that came from another place. His voice box was the instrument from which the transmission freely flowed.

Stephan chuckles to himself as he recalls a poignant moment when he pulled out all the stops by using a dramatic courtroom tactic he once saw in a movie.

He had over fifty of his volunteers in ready in the hallway outside the assembly room, loaded down with thousands of the written testimonials of UFO and extraterrestrial encounters generated by the masses of people from all walks of life.

On cue these deliverers of knowledge entered en masse, pushing and pulling wheeled metal pallets overflowing with undeniable evidence.

It was Stephan's intent to belay the question "Are they here?" The focus could now be directed on the "Why".

At the conclusion of his speech, he wasn't prepared for the deafening roar of applause that followed as the assembly rose to their feet in unison with undeniable approval. The applause was but a small token of the genuine acceptance that was to follow.

After what seemed to be an hour of congratulatory backslapping, with an abundance of kudos and accolades, Stephan remembers gathering his notes in preparation to find Liz and head back to their hotel for celebration and a much deserved rest.

Before he could leave the podium, two very high-profiled political figures approached him and offered their congratulations, which by itself filled him with pride. But what followed next was more than Stephan could have ever imagined. They proposed an immediate meeting with Stephan to discuss and formulate a plan of action to develop a unified coalition group that would be governed by the people, a cross-section humanitarian committee of his choosing, with the intent of being ready to interact with the Galactic Federation when they were sure of the people's commitment of cooperation for the good of all.

For what happens here on Earth is far-reaching into the galaxy and perhaps beyond. There are many species from distant star regions who have been watching and waiting to see how humanity utilizes the tools of higher consciousness, which is ever expanding in an effort to change and ultimately eliminate its course of environmental self-destruction, as its impact is infinite.

With this last thought, Stephan, still sitting in the chair by the window, drifts off into a deep, peaceful slumber. He is complete. Job well done!

Completing his speech before the World Council of the Humanities was exhausting enough for Stephan, but he has chosen this moment in time to introduce Liz to his family, as she has become more than a colleague in this endeavor — this mission — to change the world as we know it.

Stephan is beginning to think that what he thought was his biggest challenge pales at the prospect of articulating the past thirty-odd years' experience to his parents. After all, they were never aware of his continued "sleepwalking" visitations or especially Lupo. For all they knew, all this nonsense ceased years ago after Dr. Ortega's death. From their standpoint, that was the end of an extremely imaginative phase of Stephan's life, most likely brought on by his traumatic beginnings as a young child in Italy.

And yet Stephan finds that his dad, of all people, is questioning him more and more about the direction he has chosen to take as — in Dad's words — "a lobbyist for UFOs is it?" Not quite. But his genuine curiosity is encouraging. Enough so that Stephan has offered to have his dad join him for a few days in Washington to visit his office and watch him go through his paces. Perhaps then his father will understand a little more... Perhaps.

The short drive from the hotel in New York to Stephan's parents' home in the upper portion of the state provides Stephan and Liz the ultimate luxury of a private audience with each other to formulate their next step. Liz seems somewhat apprehensive about meeting Stephan's family. She's worried they may perceive her as another weirdo who enables Stephan to continue his unusual quest for truth. Perhaps they're right after all.

Exactly how much should Stephan reveal about his relationship with Liz, in terms of their special talents? Running the risk of Stephan's mom fainting dead on the floor and his dad reaching for whatever his hands land on in the liquor cabinet gives them pause regarding their course of action.

It's not long before they arrive at their destination. Liz appears impressed with the loveliness of the neighborhood and the pristine landscape of Stephan's childhood home, obviously produced by the caring hands of his dad, who — according to Stephan — loves to get his hands dirty and is always planting and pruning his small estate.

As they exit the car and open the trunk to retrieve their bags, Stephan's mom comes running out the front door, apron flapping in the breeze as she speeds forward in typical elderly shuffle to greet them.

"She looks wonderful," Stephan says more to himself than to Liz.

"Hey there, young man!" a voice booms from the open garage door. Stephan's dad emerges with a gardening tool in one hand and nothing in the other but the promise of a hug.

After embraces and introductions, the two couples excitedly enter the foyer of Stephan's first real home. How he's missed this place. Even with the passage of time and all the renovations over the years, the house retains its essence of home — His home.

The visit is a good one. Meeting Liz is a dream come true for Stephan's parents, who want nothing more than for their son to settle down with a nice girl and raise a family. While they may be, indeed, headed in that direction, for now Stephan and Liz have a full plate before them that takes precedence over all other personal future plans.

Stephan earnestly vows to his parents and to himself to visit more often, and Liz assures them all she'll make it her mission to see that he keeps that promise.

All too soon it's time to head back to Washington and to what lies in wait. Coming home was the best thing Stephan could have done for himself, for he knows that his mission is really just beginning. The past three and a half decades are but the preamble for what is to come.

Riding back in the car Liz finds it impossible to keep her eyes open, so she slips off to sleep. Stephan lovingly looks over at her in her peaceful slumber, the ever confident passenger trusting there's a competent driver at the wheel. Metaphor? You bet!

LOUISE ROSE AVENI

IMAGINE
© 1971 by John Lennon

Imagine there's no heaven
It's easy if you try
No hell below us
Above us only sky
Imagine all the people
Living for today...

Imagine there's no countries
It isn't hard to do
Nothing to kill or die for
And no religion too
Imagine all the people
Living life in peace...

You may say I'm a dreamer
But I'm not the only one
I hope someday you'll join us
And the world will be as one

Imagine no possessions
I wonder if you can
No need for greed or hunger
A brotherhood of man
Imagine all the people
Sharing all the world...

You may say I'm a dreamer
But I'm not the only one
I hope someday you'll join us
And the world will live as one

Epilogue (Final Word)

When I first sat down to write this book, I decided, due to the subject matter at hand, the reader would accept the events as they unfolded more easily if the book was deemed a work of fiction rather than if it had been written in a different genre.

After all, we are still processing and absorbing the plethora of materials that are available to us in so many formats, i.e., television, movies, books, Internet, and seminars relative to the existence of UFOs and E.T.'s.

Upon the book's completion, I was then struck with the quandary of whether or not to divulge even more information for the reader to consider relative to the plausibility of these events actually occurring, or should it remain the product of this author's wild imagination attempting to debunk the government's denial of the existence of these entities and their intended interaction with humanity?

Once I revisited the question, the answer was undeniable.

I needed to share with you, the reader, that many of the events portrayed in this book were, indeed, artistic recreations of actual happenings, and that the main character Stephan is loosely fashioned after a real person I knew who shared his amazing beginnings with me.

We were first introduced at his place of business in Florida right after my move from Boston, Massachusetts, in 1993. I found him to be a well-grounded individual, a respected businessman in his community, and a devoted family man.

Our casual conversations ultimately revealed a shared profound interest in "other" intangible things, such as angels, E.T.'s and UFOs. As time passed, he became more aware of my sincere exploration of the UFO and E.T. phenomena, and eventually felt comfortable enough to confide in me about his true identity and his own close encounters. His judgment was sound, as I remained open and accepting of the possibilities which piqued his desire to share even more amazing details of his Earth life. So intriguing was his story that I commented on how his would make a terrific book of fiction, and I would like to be the one to write it.

Having already shared some of my previous writing efforts with him, he expressed his admiration concerning my literary integrity and so, with his permission and encouragement, agreed to let me weave an imaginary tale with the stipulation that I honor his request to keep his identity a secret. So it was that we began our weekly Sunday afternoon meetings where I took copious notes and was allowed to tape his dialogues to assist me in formulating a viable story, with the hope of producing an epic impact upon the reader.

What impressed me most was this man's matter-of-fact recounting of his early life detailing events and encounters that were anything but normal by anyone's perspective. He was not seeking notoriety, nor was it his intention to shock me. He trusted me enough to unveil his unusual human life experiences while still a young boy, perhaps with a prophetic knowledge that I would one day write about all of this.

We both hoped the rise in mass consciousness had finally reached a level of elevation so that people would accept the possibility of a character, such as Stephan, as one of many who have walked among us since the beginning of time.

It was my intention to put a non-threatening, three-dimensional, humanoid face to those star beings living among us, in an effort to quantify their universal mission and focus, and for us to take care in our interaction with other species so as not to upset the balance of a, so far, peaceful coexistence.

Regrettably, I lost contact with this amazing being, and so took poetic license to conclude the possibilities.

I hope that one day he'll have the opportunity to read this story — and we will find ourselves, once again, in each other's experience, so that he can fill me in on his latest adventures. Sequel? Perhaps…

Wolf Wisdom

One evening, an old Cherokee told his grandson about a battle that goes on inside people. He said, "My son, the battle is between two 'wolves' inside us all."

"One is *Evil*. It is anger, jealousy, sorrow, regret, greed, arrogance, self-pity, guilt, resentment, inferiority, lies, false pride, superiority, and ego."

"The other is *Good*. It is joy, peace, love, hope, serenity, humility, kindness, benevolence, empathy, generosity, truth, compassion, and faith."

The grandson thought about it for a minute and then asked his grandfather – "Which wolf wins?"

The old Cherokee simply replied – "The one you feed."

Author Unknown

About The Author

A native of Boston, Massachusetts, Louise Rose Aveni is the youngest of three children and the only girl. She was brought up in a loving family that supported and encouraged her creative talents. At the age of five she typically explored the world of ballet and piano but found her literary voice began taking center stage by age eight.

Through her years of academia, she continued to hone her writing skills but kept them to herself, sharing her stories and poems, only, with her doting parents.

It wasn't until her bout with cancer in the mid 80's that she found her true literary voice.

Simultaneously, as her spirituality awakened, a long time curiosity with the idea of life on other planets and inter-dimensional realms gave rise to a renewed passion to explore the possibilities in earnest.

No longer concerned with how she would be perceived in her pursuit of obtaining answers to her own core questions, Louise Rose penned her first novel titled *"Lupo- Conversations with an E.T"*, which is a tapestry of fact and artistic creativity, compiled from a blend of personalities and actual events.

LUPO- Conversations with an E.T. is the first of a trilogy sequel, with *HYBRID* and *KRYSTAL*, slated for later release.

"It is my intention to take the fear factor out the subject by placing a non-threatening, benevolent face to the star beings who have, most likely, walked among us since the beginning of time."

The debut of *"Lupo – Conversations with and E.T."* is deliberately coordinated with the 60th anniversary of the 1947 UFO incident in Roswell, New Mexico and provides a plausible answer to the question *"Are they here?"* with *"Why they are here"*

Louise Rose will be traveling around the country providing interactive speaking engagements for those of like mind who are open to the possibilities.

She currently resides in Sarasota, Florida and works as a national freelance Marketing Consultant, specializing in product marketing and promotion and frequently travels to Sedona, Arizona to partake of its unprecedented beauty and commiserate with the abundance of free thinkers.

Find out more about Louise and upcoming books and events at *www.sedonaangels.com*

Printed in the United States
76799LV00005B/367-414